Duncan Swindells

BIRTH OF A SPY

Cover designed by Rob Williams at ilovemycover.com

This book is a work of fiction. Names, characters, places, and incidents either are products of the author's imagination or are used fictitiously. Any resemblance to actual persons, living or dead, events, or locales is entirely coincidental.

Please follow me @dafswindells

First Printing: February 2019

ISBN- 9781794246430

Acknowledgements

I should like to take this opportunity to thank the following;

Dr. Alison Turner for helping me when she should have been enjoying her holiday.

Lena Zeliszewska for checking my Polish.

Rob Williams from ILMC for his friendship and yet another beautiful and stylish front cover.

Terry Boyd for her excellent taste in Christmas books and gifting me the idea.

Grant Boyd for his encyclopedic knowledge of the fine arts.

My mum for being a truly great writer and reading and re-reading passages until they must have lost all meaning.

Leo, Corin and Georgia for their endless patience and support.

Prologue

If childbirth had been the gift of life, then what she wondered would death prove to be? Absolution? The redemption she'd hoped but dared not pray for? At the least she supposed, a peaceful and never-ending sleep. She'd made sure the house had been empty before fetching the length of coiled grey electrical cable from its cupboard beneath the stairs. In the hallway she'd caught herself in the tall and damning giltwood mirror which hung by the door examining her profile. She gently pushed at her fragile blonde hair, feeling it bounce back into place under the duress of that morning's generously applied hairspray. Seeing herself again like that, in the mirror as the questions persisted only threatened to strengthen her resolve. She smiled thinly, her mouth tired and quavering.

Carefully, so there would be no mistake, she set about fastening the cable to the brass door handle which opened into the sitting room, twisting it this way, pulling it that, checking it was secure. The back of her hand travelled across her face, absently wiping away another tear. She would not look in the mirror again. She went to throw the cable over the door, succeeding only at the second attempt. One final inspection of her handiwork followed by a strange moment of pride;

the knot would hold. Another hand across her damp cheek before closing, then locking the door firmly behind her, her hand spotted and flecked from the freshly applied mascara. Then she was pulling the cable taught through the ill-fitting doorframe. She had never wanted to live in an old house, that had always been his idea. They were so difficult to keep and cold in the winter too. Taking a chair from their dining set she carefully positioned it next to the door. Now for the other knot. She held the cable in a loose S, wrapping it back and around. Two, three attempts before it met her satisfaction. She slipped out of her shoes, arranging them neatly by the door and in stockinged feet stepped up onto the chair, facing the room. *Her* room, *her* home, *her* family. She checked her blouse, her pearls and smoothed down her skirt, re-arranging an errant pleat, then, trying not to disturb her hair, slipped the noose over her head and gently began to rock the chair. Her family she thought, it had always been her family, well now it was time to put an end to all of that. She felt the cold plastic cable by her ear as the chair tipped and slid away from her. An end to the memories. An end to the pain and the guilt.

As her feet skidded on the highly polished leather she felt the bight of the noose. Soon everything would be better. Soon it would be over and he would be gone. Her foot slid off the edge of the chair as it rocked and tumbled out of control, the woman's arms shooting out from her sides in an involuntary and unwanted closing gesture of self-preservation.

She lost consciousness almost immediately, her hands instinctively clawing as the cable tightened around her neck. And then, in one final act of wanton self-destruction, unable or unwilling to maintain her balance, a flailing foot kicked the chair from beneath her.

The cable whipped and flexed, straining hard against the sitting room door and then, under extreme pressure, the brass fittings buckled and twisted. First one and then with a harsh wrench, all of the soft metal screws deformed and tore from their mountings sending showers of splintered pine into the hallway. The handle flew upwards towards its frame as the woman's writhing body dropped. The chair, kicked violently, sent crashing against an old and unloved oak cabinet. The sound of shattering glass, the acrid smell of urine as, her neck neatly broken, her body failed her. She lost her grip on the cable and then just as the last of her strength was about to abandon her, one final convulsive spasm.

She came to rest on the carpeted floor, her body crumpled next to the upturned chair. And that was how they would find her.

1

Scott Hunter was conscious, all be it somewhat reluctantly, suspended in a somnolent limbo between the horrors of the sleeping world and the inconvenient yet ever present realities of the waking one. He'd woken alone, wearily regarding the vacant side of their bed and silently thanking her for not rousing him. He'd slept terribly, again, waking often, until finally at 2 o'clock, as he did most every night, he had given up and slipped from their bed to wander the house in search of distraction. He'd sat at the kitchen table, powerless to read a word of the paper which lay open in front of him. Awake enough to be unable to sleep, but not enough to be able to function meaningfully, he'd wondered about making a hot drink but had instead found himself staring torpidly into unavailing space.

As a teenager Hunter had experienced a sudden and quite profound physical and nervous breakdown. There followed a prolonged and uncomfortable sojourn at the local children's hospital where he had been prescribed a cocktail of drugs; Citalopram for the depression, Valium for his nerves and Temazepam for the sleepless nights. These had only succeeded in dulling his normally sharp wits and, ironically, causing him the intermittent yet chronic insomnia by which, nearly ten years later, he was still affected.

Closing the paper Hunter slipped back upstairs, intent on examining his laptop, but then, not wanting to wake Amy had thought better of it and returned, past his snoring flatmate's bedroom, downstairs to the sitting room and the television, the kitchen now out of bounds, in Hunter's mind complicit in his wakefulness. Idly he'd flicked through a handful of channels, but in the early hours of the morning all that appeared available was a Hobson's choice of televised gambling and documentaries about Hitler, aliens or often some obscenely far-fetched combination of the two. Finally, exhausted by his own exhaustion, and in danger of falling uncomfortably asleep on the couch, he had gingerly returned to bed. Amy had snuffled ominously but, he was relieved to see, had not woken.

Now it was mid-morning and he was determined to salvage the remainder of the day. He'd showered but not shaved, thrown on an old Bauhaus t-shirt and a pair of skinny black jeans but no socks. With the house empty and a freshly brewed cup of coffee at his elbow Scott Hunter slid the MacBook from his khaki messenger bag and placed it on the desk. The ad had said the bag would be tough and durable, but already its stitching was beginning to fray and it would probably be long outlived by its contents. Hunter couldn't afford for his computer to be damaged but until he found some work he couldn't afford the price of a new shoulder bag either. He removed the silver laptop from its soft protective case and carefully lifted the lid. The machine sprang to life, displaying the last program he'd left running. He watched with pleasure as figures tumbled down the screen. A steady stream of numbers broken only by the occasional blank lending the page its peculiar rolling rhythm. Hunter sipped his coffee and thought about the hours, no the days spent writing this program. Having recently left university, he was now able to code purely for sheer pleasure and not for the gratification of his lecturers. Consequently this programme had satisfied him more than any other of his undergraduate assignments; a complete indulgence, of no use to anyone but himself and an extremely select few.

Hunter had always been fascinated by codes. From an early age, whilst his peers had kicked at a football or each other he'd poured over anything and everything his limited yet earnest provincial library could muster on the subject, from the hieroglyphs of the Old Kingdom to Al-Kindi's 8th century masterpiece *Manuscript for the Deciphering of Cryptographic Messages*, the procurement of which had caused no end of raised eyebrows and handwringing from the libraries chief librarian. He read about the various cyphers employed by The Papal States, and then in the nineteenth century the pioneering work of Charles Babbage and the Prussian Friedrich Kasiski. He devoured Edgar Allan Poe. Then one day, quite by chance, he'd found an article in his father's newspaper about a hitherto unrecognised and highly secretive establishment which had only recently thrown open its doors to the general public. Hunter had insisted on visiting Bletchley Park the very next weekend and soon knew everything there was to know about the work carried out there, how ten thousand men and women had laboured tirelessly through the Second World War, to break message after message sent using an extraordinary machine christened Enigma by the Allies. Hunter had found himself seduced by the world of the Special Operations Executive and the OSS. Allan Turin became an unlikely teenage hero.

And then as he'd delved deeper and deeper into the world of cryptographic analysis and his mathematical gifts had begun to be recognised Hunter realised that he saw and felt numbers differently from other people. To his private delight he would follow in the footsteps of so many of his heroes. Cambridge beckoned.

Writing an advanced hill climbing algorithm for no other reason than to break messages sent more than fifty years before Hunter's birth had just been a bit of fun. Initially he'd worked on codes which had already been broken, but that hadn't lessened his satisfaction as it allowed him to compare his workings with the greatest minds of the 1940s. The algorithm started with an arbitrary solution and incrementally sought to improve upon it, changing one element after another at each turn. Then, when the algorithm came upon an improvement it would make this new solution its starting point and begin all over again, eventually arriving at a local optimum or a solution upon which it could not improve. But since those early programs Hunter had written increasingly more and more sophisticated ones, finally succeeding in breaking a message that had previously gone unsolved by Bletchley Park, GCHQ or anybody else since 1945. It's content, once revealed had proven prosaic and mundane but that hadn't mattered. For Hunter it had been the crowning vindication of his algorithm's superiority over all other competition.

Slightly to his annoyance, this achievement had earned him a brief moment of unwanted fame amongst his fellow students, with a couple of column inches in one of the less popular broad sheets. On the back of Hunter's success a college professor had established a club and encouraged other prodigies to write their own software. The club was still active, but when people had started talking about committees and sub-committees Hunter had quickly lost interest. Instead he'd joined a small hardcore community of online enthusiasts spread around the globe. Hunter had never actually met or spoken to any of them in person, preferring to communicate solely through chat rooms and emails, an arrangement which suited him very well.

As line after line of code continued to tumble down the screen, and with, for the moment his work largely done, Hunter wondered whether the other members of his select little band had jobs, commitments, bills to pay or mouths to feed. Not for the first time Enigma was proving a convenient distraction. He stared out of their bedroom window at the calm Cambridge street below, remembering the day they had agreed to live together. Then, as his programme continued to toil in the background, he recalled the day they had moved into the house. Hunter's thoughts were about to leave him behind altogether when the sight of a smartly dressed man not significantly older than himself, carrying a briefcase and marching past on the opposite side of the street with a sense of purpose Hunter could only wonder at, dragged him back to his own workaday reality. He must do something meaningful before Amy returned.

He was just about to open an internet browser and commence the ever tedious search for employment when the programme he'd been running abruptly stopped. Now no longer the algorithm's rolling numbers but a page of letters, grouped in fours and seemingly in an utterly random order. These were the original Enigma codes. After some research Hunter was confident that the message his algorithm had been struggling to break had originated from a weather monitoring station somewhere in the North Sea, and had been sent in the last few months of the war. The Mac's arrow hovered over the decode tab and he clicked the mouse pad. The arrow was briefly replaced by a spinning progress indicator before the letters unravelled and to his delight Hunter saw half a dozen German words smeared together into one long and incomprehensible sentence. Languages had never been his strong point but he quickly recognised the words for wind and temperature. The rest would have to wait until his house mate returned from college. As Hunter looked at the rich German text he couldn't help but wonder what Amy's reaction would be. No doubt she'd be dismissively unimpressed and ask why he was wasting his valuable time with such nonsense. He took the page from his Brother Printer and slid it inside the MacBook's protective soft case next to the laptop. The more he thought about Amy the more, reluctantly, he had to admit that she was probably right. He couldn't carry on like this for much longer. He did need a job. However, that would all have to wait. With a freshly broken code in his shoulder bag, Hunter's only real concern was how quickly he could be at the university.

Before catching the bus into town he dropped in on his local newsagents and bought copies of The Times and, as something of an afterthought, The Cambridge News, in a half-hearted attempt at appeasing Amy. Standing at the bus stop outside the little parade of faded local shops he opened the Cambridge paper. One quick look at the jobs section was enough to confirm his worst fears. There were column after column of people looking for plumbers, cooks, cleaners and day carers. There was even, he noted with a raised eyebrow, a secretarial position at his old college which paid poorly, but better than he had imagined it might. But no one was recruiting for a maths graduate with a 2-1 or any other kind of degree. He knew Amy's feelings on the subject. *Get out there and earn some money. Pursue your dream job later.* Well, that was fine for her, she had walked out of college and straight into employment. A job she'd wanted too, in marketing. What, Hunter wondered, the hell were you supposed to do with a 2-1 in mathematics? What for that matter was his "dream job"? and why, in all the years of study and academic endeavour had no one spent the least bit of time with him discussing what he was to do with his hard-earned qualifications? He flicked through the remainder of the paper. A section of dual carriageway was due to be closed until November, inconveniencing local residents terribly and Hunter suspected for considerably longer than the six months stated, The Council was preparing to unveil a new and hopefully improved recycling initiative and the Dean of his old college had been involved in a sex scandal. Hunter really couldn't have cared less about any of it, least of all the sex scandal. He'd only ever met the man twice and the second time had been at his graduation. The bus pulled into Drummer Street Station.

Sir John Alperton let a sun-washed hand fall down the crease in his trousers. His tailors had excelled themselves this time. He flicked his long legs crossed and admired the highly polished toecap of his black shoe. Not cheap, but worth every penny. His father had always told him you could judge a great deal about a chap from the shoes that he wore. Strange to think of the old man. Well, what would he have had to say about his son now? In spite of, or perhaps because of the Jermyn Street shirts, the suits from Savile Row and even the shoes, lovingly handmade in a naturally evasive little Etruscan hilltop village sleeping quietly, deep in the heart of rural Tuscany, he could picture the look of barely disguised contempt his father's face would have worn. Not at the titles, the decorations or any of the other trappings, the shoes, the suits, the handmade silk ties, not even at the regular marital infidelities. No, it was the nature of his son's work which had so offended the old man. He'd paid his debt after all. He'd worked at a proper job, he'd got his hands properly dirty by doing proper hard graft not from sitting behind a desk in Whitehall.

Alperton still wore the old man's belt from time to time. The object that had inflicted the punishments had ironically helped in some small part shape him into the man he had become. So now when he wore the belt, it was not through any perverse sense of self-loathing following the years of beatings, first at his father's hands and then The Sisters of Mercy. Quite the opposite. A feeling of closeness, familiarity, even solidarity. Of being encompassed by the very thing that had surrounded his own father for so many years. In any case, now he had his own offspring to feel disappointed with. Strange to think of him now though.

Sir John's head fell back, tilting slightly towards the sun, momentarily causing him to squint. He removed a cigarette from its pack and lit it, thinking what a rare treat it was to be able to smoke without being made to feel like a social pariah. Hard for him to believe, but he couldn't even smoke in his own office anymore and had to go and stand in a huddle of cleaners and backroom staff. Times had certainly changed. Through the smoke he watched a family of tourists. American he presumed from their clothing and their body language. The children were horsing around in front of Frampton's statue of Peter Pan whilst a dowdy wife gave an overweight husband instructions on how to take the kid's photograph with an iPad. No, not Americans. Canadians. Wherever they were from, their progeny were boisterous and noisy and just at that particular moment, quite unwanted. Their place, he was pleased to see, taken by a young couple, their heads reverentially bowed to read the brass plate of explanation at the statue's base.

Sir John Alperton looked away, over The Serpentine. Moorhens were noisily pecking at the weeds and each other as, further out geese patrolled in pairs. Geese. He hated geese, except at Christmas, of course. He would have to watch his step around here if he were to avoid their poisonous green shit. Perched on one of the many sturdy wooden structures erupting from the lake, their purpose unknown to him, an equally mystifying tall thin black bird, sitting quite still and imperious whilst in the distance faded green and white deck chairs pushed and pulled in the spring breeze and indolent cranes slipped gracefully between church steeples. If it weren't for the geese and the damn tourists, even the Canadian ones Sir John reflected sadly, Hyde Park could be Heaven.

Another puff on his cigarette and then he'd consult his watch. It was unlike him to be late and he'd picked this spot because it was only a short walk from the man's apartment. But then on reflection the gentleman he had arranged to meet must be quite elderly by now. In truth he hadn't seen him for a number of years although there had been a time when they had regularly shared drinks at Sir John's club in Knightsbridge. He supposed the man's advancing years had put paid to that too. The Canadians had gone he realised with relief, the boy teasing his sister whilst their parents struggled to open a street map of London. He stubbed out his cigarette on top of the bin at his elbow and sat back on the park bench, scanning the horizon against the low sun. Peering into the distance he caught sight of the man, causing him, involuntarily, to consult his wrist watch. A slight, hunched figure wearing an overcoat in the centre of London on a sultry spring evening, the man seemed to be doing his level best to arouse suspicion. At a second glance Sir John realised he appeared to be playing cricket, or at least returning a ball to a group of young Asian lads who were enthusiastically putting willow to leather. Their ball had come to rest in his path and he stooped and, with a little effort, threw it back to them. There was pride in that delivery. A glimpse of the elderly man's youth, of sticky summer Sundays, flat warm beer and limited overs. The throw wasn't challenging, it was offering. I'm one of you it said, or used to be. But for the passage of time and, Sir John recalled, a brief spell under the surgeon's knife which had robbed him of much of his peripheral vision, we might be friends, adversaries, combatants over twenty-two yards.

Sir John had picked this spot so the old boy wouldn't overexert himself. As he drew closer Alperton slid along the bench to create more room. Ah, a brogue. Of course. A distinguished old mahogany brogue, well-kept and Sir John presumed, regularly returned to its original last. A solid, dependable, honest shoe. Well, what had his father known anyway? All this proved was that appearances could be deceptive. Honesty, as well as any number of other traits could and regularly were bought. And every man, despite what they might tell you to the contrary, did have his price. The elderly gentleman took a cautious glance around, reached under his coat and produced a thick Manilla envelope which he placed in the middle of the bench before creakily sitting down at the other end. Sir John shot him a conspiratorial smile. A pair of old troopers from a bygone age enjoying one last act of tradecraft. He picked up the envelope, ran a manicured hand down the thigh of his trousers and was on his way. The whole exchange had taken seconds.

Through time Professor Freddie Sinclair had developed his own understated yet distinctive dress code and he wore it now; ivory slacks, a linen jacket dancing loosely over a delicately checked shirt endorsing a dark monochrome knitted woollen tie, usually green. Hunter noted the shoes, only worn by men of a certain age; a dusty sailor-boy blue, with laces so incidental they were almost a slip-on. They looked comfortable whilst simultaneously appearing asexual and effete, their cream rubber soles as softly spoken as their host. Sinclair's hair was silver and cropped short. He liked to boast quietly that he'd been visiting the same barbers every fortnight since his appointment at the university almost thirty years ago. A product of the Grammar school system, Hunter suspected that, even though he was preeminent in his field, some of the other lecturers, brimming with their easy sense of over entitlement, did not always credit Professor Sinclair with the respect he was due. Hunter was certain there was an old boys network for the so called "Great Public Schools" of Eton, Harrow, Charterhouse and the like and that, try as he might, Sinclair would never be accepted and he knew it.

'Welcome,' he said with a careworn smile.

Hunter let the warmth of the professor's study envelop him, the familiar smell of old books, warm leather and rising above it all the faintest aroma of lemon and weak tea. The professor's walls were covered with neo-classical scenes in antiquity, David, Ingres and Hunter's personal favourite, Moreau's Meeting of the Sphinx. Amongst the prints and the many trappings of academia, the framed citations and first editions, and scattered respectfully between the great masters, the professor's own forays into the world of art. Watercolours of the beach at Aldburgh, a sloop picked out against the setting sun in delicately applied sable. Snape, The Maltings, each perfectly realised yet next to Delacroix and Courbet sadly insipid and inert. On one wall a long oak shelf set aside solely for the professor's diaries. A line of identical black leather-bound note books which Hunter knew to contain unlined pages, their corners elegantly clipped on an angle and always bought from the same tiny independent bookshop. Hunter wondered whether, if for any reason the shop should stop selling them, or worse still go out of business altogether, the professor would be able to continue? Only on rare occasions had he ever witnessed Sinclair make an entry. He would reverentially draw down the current year, sometimes pausing to re-read a previous day's deliberations before, in the same dull black ink of his paintings, writing in his flawless hand, a hand so particular and uniform that Hunter felt incapable of reading more than a few sentences. It wasn't hard for him to imagine that, once the professor had gone, his diaries might be read and even published, but Hunter did not envy the scholar who undertook such a task. Sinclair stood by his desk toying expectantly with his fine rimless spectacles.

'Well Scott, were we right? A weather report?'

Hunter nodded slowly, enjoying the drama and eager to retain some last semblance of ownership before handing over his latest discovery.

'I've not seen Joth today, but even with my schoolboy German it seems to be a report from a weather station.'

'Norway?'

'Possibly.' His last chance. Once the code ceased to be a jumble of meaningless letters and reverted to its original German, Hunter's work was done and it fell completely under Sinclair's eager ownership.

'I knew it. Are you thinking Svalbard and Spitsbergen?'

Hunter smiled and it was gone. The professor was so desperate to place the origin of the transmission on the Norwegian archipelago. There had been so much speculation regarding its on-off existence as a Nazi base. This could confirm it once and for all and in the small community of amateur historians Sinclair inhabited, that would be considered something of a coup.

'Let's just wait until I've spoken to Joth and we've had a closer look at some of the co-ordinates,' Hunter cautioned.

Professor Sinclair however had made up his mind and moved on. He turned to the mirror above his writing desk, removed his spectacles and carefully ran a comb through his thinning silver-grey hair.

'I knew it. Spitsbergen,' he said reaching for his student's latest reward.

***

Hunter sat on the top deck of the bus back to his bedsit, in his hand the new set of Enigma codes Professor Sinclair had given him. Sometimes the professor was unable to immediately obtain his next challenge and there would be a frustrating wait whilst letters were written and clandestine phone calls made, but on this occasion there had been no such delay and Hunter found himself staring at two sheets of photocopied paper. Two new messages to be de-coded. He looked at the corresponding groups, trying to breathe fresh life and meaning to them and wondering what secrets they held. Another weather station perhaps or maybe this time they were from a U-boat? One that had been depth charged and forced to dive. Fancifully he let his mind roam and play. Troop movements on the Western Front, a tank battle in the African desert, the prospect of Nazi gold, stolen works of art or other unimaginable treasures. The reality would probably be infinitely more mundane, a routine communications check relaying that everything was as it had been the day before. And then there was always the chance it would be the traffic he hoped he'd never read.

Train times and destinations. Numbers of people dispatched. Numbers received. Numbers processed.

Even before he opened the front door Hunter could hear Amy and Joth's raised voices. Another lively political debate no doubt. Joth was the new breed of South African, brimming with confidence, bullish and outdoorsy in a way which made Hunter heartily sick, but politically reconstituted, open minded and having grown up under Mandela, charmingly naive and idealistic. Hunter had first met him in The Fountain, the pair hitting it off immediately. The abuse, the banter, on Joth's country of birth or his nation's cricket or rugby teams had never let up in the three years they had lived together. Amy was debating the pros and cons of positive discrimination as Hunter entered the kitchen. Joth, bleached hair, deep olive tan and Boardriders t-shirt was literally being backed into a corner. Hunter winced. She was advancing on him with a raised finger and a mug of steaming coffee. She shot him a look. I'm nearly finished here, it said, I'll deal with you in a minute, before returning to harangue his flatmate. Hunter knew better than to try and intercede and so drew up a kitchen chair and, like a celebrity at a prize fight, waited to see who would draw first blood.

Amy was fierce and wonderful when she was like this. She was only a couple of inches over five feet tall but that made her no less formidable. Today, complementing her charcoal grey skirt and jacket she wore a pair of black suede ankle boots that gave her an extra inch. She cracked her coffee mug down on the table next to Hunter and ran both hands through her long dark hair. Hunter almost felt sorry for Joth. Amy was just about to make good her point when abruptly, catching herself, she stopped and rounded on him.

'Your father phoned.'

'Okay. Thanks.' She looked down at him, the dark hazel eyes that he loved so much suddenly soft and pleading.

'Come on Scott. He wants to know how you are.'

'Well I'm fine, aren't I?'

'Great,' she said shaking her head, 'very mature.'

He knew what she was trying to do. Why wouldn't she just let it go? He wasn't interested in reconciliation, some wounds ran too deep and whatever they might tell you to the contrary, time was not always the great healer. She didn't understand, but this was the way it had been for years now and this, Hunter thought with only a slight twinge of regret, was the way it would remain. Out of the corner of his eye he watched as Joth tried to slink out of the kitchen, but Hunter wasn't about to let him escape that easily.

'I've got another code for you.'

Amy looked away. She'd heard enough, long since having tired of his obsession.

*** ***

In their bedroom Hunter slid the MacBook from its protective cover and onto the table by the window, letting the magnetic power cable snap into place, the machine's green light blinking on. Quickly he called up the algorithm, examining it with paternal pride. He took down a blue ring binder from the shelves which ran down his side of the bed and carefully shook the new codes from the anonymous brown envelope Sinclair had given him. Now when he studied the documents he was no longer looking at the Enigma code but searching for any other information the pages might yield.

It was not unusual for the professor to obtain them directly from Bletchley Park. Hunter had never liked to ask because the one time he had hinted at the subject he'd received an uncharacteristically frosty rebuke. He suspected though, that they had to have come from one of the museum's curators. Clearly although most of the material was declassified there was still a huge amount of secrecy surrounding both Enigma and Station X. All the nearly ten thousand men and women who had worked there had signed the official secrets act and all, with only a handful of exceptions had abided by it right through to the nineteen-seventies when the existence of Bletchley Park had first been acknowledged. Even so, much of the material from Bletchley had remained a closely guarded secret well into the new millennium.

Hunter took in the familiar War Office insignia and the professor's immaculately handwritten suggestion that the message, in his opinion, could be Italian in origin. He noted that much of the usual information had been redacted many years before. The documents, photocopies, were covered in marks and date stamps which, had Hunter been more interested, would have told him their journey from locked filing cabinet to locked filing cabinet. Unusually they appeared to have come from the Imperial War Museum and not Bletchley Park, but this wasn't of any great concern to Hunter either. He was looking for clues as to the dates and locations of their original transmission. Either of these would help narrow down the model of machine used to encrypt the messages and aid an educated guess as to its many settings. The messages had been intercepted in 1942 which indicated they could have only been sent by a small number of Enigma machines, which in turn meant fewer wheels, fewer cables, fewer permutations and with a little luck a quicker resolution.

As he started to make the necessary adjustments to his algorithm Hunter ran the A4 sheets through his scanner. Only fair to share. The new scans pinged onto his desktop, he opened his account and prepared to send a group email. Once the JPEGs were attached he typed;

Latest from the Prof.
Think one might be Italian?
Good Luck. SH

and clicked send. The email whooshed from his Outbox to the group's seven recipients. Next he sent the file to the Brother Laser Printer which quickly churned out two more hard copies. Hunter rifled through a drawer of pens and pencils, finding an old calculator, its battery long dead, a half-finished course of sleeping tablets and under a hole punch, a pad of lurid pink post it notes.

3rd May 2012, IWM? 14th June 1942 Italy?

He stuck the note to the top right corner of the copy, punched a couple of holes down one side and placed the page carefully with the others in his blue ring binder. Hunter was just about to check on the algorithm's progress when he felt a hand on his shoulder. He had been so wrapped up in his work he'd failed to hear Amy enter. She planted a conciliatory kiss on the top of his head.

'Sorry,' he said without looking up or really meaning it.

She ruffled his already messy hair.

'When are you going to talk to him? He worries about you.'

No response. This, Hunter knew, was the real reason she had come. Not to see how he was, but to badger him about his father.

'So do I, as it happens,' she continued as if reading his mind.

Still no response, but now that she'd said she was worried about him Hunter forced himself to turn and face her.

'Have you got any further with...' Amy stopped herself. Hunter had started to frown. She had jumped from one difficult topic to the next without hesitating, even though she knew it was not the way to handle him.

'I bought the bloody paper,' he snapped surprised by his own anger, 'but if you really want me to go and sweep the streets then fine.'

'Jesus. No one's suggesting...' Why did it have to be like this every time either subject was raised?

'I just think that might be a bit of waste of my degree?' Hunter put in unhelpfully.

My degree. My degree. Why was it always about his bloody degree? Amy was beginning to wish she had never broached the subject. She had studied too, graduated too. Why was she being made to feel guilty for putting her qualifications to good use? In fact, why was she being made to feel guilty at all? Perhaps marketing wasn't such a noble pursuit but she was damned if she was having *that* debate again.

'Yes, Scott,' she replied wearily, 'I said, no one is suggesting that.'

Impasse. Stalemate. Amy took her hand from his hair and moved to the window. If she was going to say what she needed to say she didn't want to have to see his reaction. Hunter continued to tap at the MacBook as if everything was fine.

'I went to see Sinclair today,' he muttered in a perfunctory attempt at changing the subject.

'About a job?' Even as Amy heard the words leave her mouth, she knew she was nagging.

'No. Not about a job.'

More awkward silence, with neither knowing quite how to continue. Amy chewed her bottom lip. She had to say it. She loved him and wanted only the best for him.

'Have you thought about giving Alec a ring?'

And there it was. Hunter let the wind go out of him. His shoulders drooped and he slid forward on his chair like a rag doll, staring at the patchy carpet between his feet.

'I was wondering when you'd bring him up,' he said trying but failing to sound buoyant.

'Oh, come on Scott, he's your friend, or at least he used to be. For Christ's sake swallow that ridiculous pride of yours and give him a ring.'

'I won't be a charity case. I don't need the help of your ex-boyfriends or anyone one else for that matter.' Hunter knew he was behaving unreasonably, but he had wanted to fire off that salvo even if it were the hollowest of victories. In fact, he realised, what he'd really wanted to do was to make the situation worse. Boyfriends, he'd said, without ever really thinking what he was implying.

'That's clever Scott, that's really bloody clever. Just remind me, you got your degree did you?' and then Amy was heading for the door. 'I'd really been looking forward to spending the evening with you, but seeing as the genius with the degree seems intent on behaving like an emotionally crippled teenager I think I'd rather go out with Joth. If that's all right with you, of course?' She didn't wait for his reply. 'And don't bother texting.'

That night, the day's events fresh in his mind and Amy's words still ringing in his ears, Hunter's insomnia had been worse than ever. After brooding some he'd continued to work at the new codes Sinclair had given him. Then, worn out and frustrated, and in danger of nodding off in front of his laptop, he'd kicked around the kitchen for a while feeling sorry for himself, careering wildly between anger and ignominy. In an effort to clear his head and with the house strangely quiet, he'd contemplated sitting up and waiting for Amy to return. He composed and then re-composed his apology, but when she didn't reply to his texts Hunter decided to call it a night. He checked his laptop before getting into bed. The algorithm was still working away at the problem and so he left the machine glowing busily on his table and tried, wholly unsuccessfully, to sleep.

Hunter wasn't sure what time it was when Joth and Amy returned. He listened as they scaled each creaking stair and then, with Amy teetering unsteadily by their bed, he pretended to sleep. Slowly she took off her top, then awkwardly eased out of her jeans, giggling with the effort. Hunter watched her in her bra and pants, her beautiful hair falling over her breasts. She took a gulp of water from the glass by their bed, then she was unhooking her bra, shaking it down her arms, letting it fall to the floor. Hunter was breathing hard as she slipped into bed next to him.

***

With Amy sleeping peacefully by his side Hunter sank once more, deep into insomnia's abusive grasp. He stared at their bedroom walls, finding new and terrifying creatures in every cheerless shadow and unlit corner. Eventually he knew he would get out of bed and prowl around the house, but for now he was desperate to cling to the suggestion of sleep. Every night there was the hope that his body would reset itself, like an unreliable clock, its cogs would suddenly align, its movement synchronize and he would fall into a blissful and unchallenged slumber, and yet every night, at exactly 2 o'clock he would tire of waiting and, angry with himself and his inability to achieve what everybody else seemed to take for granted, would capitulate. This evening however his routine, such as it was, had been disturbed. He watched the glowing figures of the clock radio next to their bed, he watched as the minutes ticked inexorably by. It was 4 o'clock in the morning and he had still not slept. Perhaps he would give Amy's DVD collection another chance, even if there wasn't a film which interested him, he thought with a crooked grin, it might help him sleep? Then there were the pills he'd discovered earlier. He left their bed and quietly opened the drawer in his desk. There they were. He couldn't tell exactly *what* they were in the dark of their room but one sleeping tablet was much the same as another. Reluctantly he made the decision and was just about to fetch a glass of water from the kitchen when he noticed the screen on his laptop light up. A new plain text. Hunter put any plans of sleep firmly and determinedly behind him. With Amy snoring drunkenly, he tapped away at his MacBook and then the Brother Printer was producing a black and white copy of the five lines. He read them through quickly to confirm that he couldn't translate them himself, threw on an old dressing gown and went into the hall and along to Joth's bedroom, the sleeping tablets reassuringly forgotten. He didn't knock. Joth never had any of his girlfriends back to stay. He made it a rule and Hunter often wondered how many of them actually knew where he lived. Confident his friend would be alone he bowled in and threw the main light switch.

'Time to go to work my little South African friend,' he said cheerfully pulling duvet and pillows from Joth's head.

'You've got to be kidding, Scott? What time is it?'

'I've got a new one. Plain text. Just came through. German.'

'Scott, it's...' Joth screwed up his eyes and tried to focus on the clock by his bed, 'Christ Scott, it's a quarter past four.'

'It's German, not Italian.'

'I don't care. Go to bed.'

'I've a feeling...'

'Scott! We both know you don't have feelings, otherwise you wouldn't be here. The only way I'm doing anything right now is if the house is on fire. Is the house on fire?'

'No.'

'Well will you please fuck off then. I'm sure there are better things you could be doing with Amy?'

The initial excitement was beginning to wear off and Hunter began to wonder if perhaps he had taken things a little too far. He placed the A4 sheet at the bottom of Joth's chaotic bed and made to leave. As he reached the door he turned back into the bedroom to check if Joth had reconsidered.

'Sod off, Scott.'

Clearly he had not.

'And turn the bloody light off.'

✳✳✳

At breakfast Amy sat in her pyjamas, her hair piled with practised indifference on top of her head, listlessly pushing a mug of coffee around whilst Hunter scrambled some eggs.

'How's the head?'

'Better than Joth's I should image. God, that boy can drink.' She took another pull on her coffee and shook her head. 'Plus I think he may have had an unwanted visitor in the night?'

'He wasn't the only one.'

'I didn't notice you complaining at the time.'

Beneath her tousled hair Amy's eyes twinkled at Hunter and he could have dragged her back to bed there and then had she not needed to go to work. A truce had definitely been declared and perhaps sensing Hunter's intentions Amy changed the subject.

'You'll think about it, won't you?' she asked as tactfully as her hangover would allow.

'What?'

'The job. Alec.'

Hunter hadn't given Alec or his job a great deal of thought because he'd never seriously contemplated approaching Amy's ex or relying on his benevolence.

'I'll think about it.'

They sat quietly and listened to the sounds of Joth coming to terms with the world before finally hauling himself out of bed.

Breakfast was nearly over when the muscular South African belatedly drew up to the table. Amy took one look at him, his bloodshot eyes, and deathly pallor and both she and Hunter burst out laughing.

'Jah, jah. Very funny waking me up in the middle of the night with your silly bloody schoolboy games.' Joth threw two pieces of paper in Hunter's direction before shakily pouring himself a coffee. 'I should charge you for those.'

Hunter snatched them up. The first was indeed from a weather station confirming that everything was as it had been the previous day. At the end of the message were temperatures, barometric readings and co-ordinates which he was happy leaving to the professor to decypher. After reading the transcript through several times Hunter felt a terrible wave of anti-climax. He eagerly took up the second sheet.

'I think you'll like that one better,' Joth spluttered through a mouthful of breakfast cereal.

Forced to submerge during attack, depth charges. Last enemy location 08:30h, Marqu AJ 9863, 220 degrees, 8 nautical miles, I am following the enemy. Barometer 1014 Millibar tendency falling, NNO 4, visibility 10.

'Now that's the sort of thing. Bloody Hell, Joth, this is actually from a U-boat. Wait until Sinclair sees this, he'll shit a brick,' and before Amy could say another word, Hunter rushed upstairs to change and, all thoughts of any job long forgotten, take the first bus into Cambridge.

✳✳✳

David stood at his kitchen window and looked out over the walled garden below. The garden which in recent years had become his own private sanctuary. The previous autumn two large trees had come down allowing in more light to the shadier areas. He'd taken great care in replanting those beds, testing and re-testing the soil before choosing plants he hoped would flourish. Then the ground had been meticulously prepared, here with lime, there potash or bone meal. In the months which followed David had created two new paths. He'd laid special cloth to keep the weeds down and then painstakingly raked over tonnes of fine pea gravel. All his hard work had been worth it and now he was able to enjoy the fruits of the previous year's labours. He took a sip of coffee and nodded slowly to himself. It was time. Everything was in place and he'd been avoiding this for far too long. He put down his coffee and considered his clothes. His top would do, he supposed, but perhaps he ought to roll up his sleeves and put on some different shoes.

A puff of dust issued from the attic as David released the hatch door, causing him instinctively to look away. He hooked a long metal rod into the legs of the extendable ladders and pulled, but this time as the ladders awkwardly descended towards him and more dust fell from the space above, he shaded his eyes. The house was nearly three hundred years old and consequently the loft space was small and cramped, initially comprising of nothing more than bare brickwork and beams, but David had worked solidly through one long hot summer to insulate and floor the area, the attic becoming his own private sauna at times. Although he hadn't been up there for years, he held a clear mental picture of where everything was to be found, right down to the electric light switch he'd screwed into a ceiling joist conveniently at arm's length. He briefly groped around before flicking the switch, the naked bulb, hanging from its joist above, flooding the room with thin pale yellow light.

Although David was confident what he would find, when his head poked above the floor and into the body of the attic he was still surprised. There were a pair of well-loved boat rods, their rings covered in cobwebs, next to them a slightly rusty and shamefully neglected set of golf clubs. When David had moved out to the country an old work colleague had suggested he take up the game, but it had never suited him. Golf, it was said, was a good walk ruined, but for David the issues were not with the game itself, but with its players. He found the many social interactions and conventions a struggle. The men were individually pleasant enough, but put them in a group and they enjoyed nothing more than to moan apologetically about their wives and crow about the money they earned in a way which David found both offensive and vulgar in equal measure. If it had purely been a case of propelling a dimpled white ball a couple of hundred yards and then into a hole with a stick, David imagined he might well have quite enjoyed the sport. It was the people who ruined it for him.

Next to the golf bag a wall of carefully stacked cardboard boxes. These he knew were full of old tax returns and documents relating to the purchase of the house. The box he was looking for had been placed somewhere on its own and not with other things. His mother's sewing machine. Old suit cases from a time when they'd travelled. A set of hi-fi speakers which, even if they still worked, would need a hell of a clean. And there, at the far end of the loft space, two cardboard boxes standing very much apart from the others. Silently cursing himself for not bringing a torch he stooped and struggling with the dark debilitating shadows cast by that one solitary bulb David was soon crouched over the boxes. The first he discounted immediately, understanding what that contained. It's neighbour he carefully prised open. Peering inside the dark void, he moved round to let as much of the limited light shine in as possible. No, not a void, a black plastic bin bag carefully wrapped in brown packing tape to keep the dust out. Yes, this was it and no further investigation was needed. He closed the box and after one last look around the space to see what other treasures languished within, turned off the light and left.

2

Professor Frederick Sinclair had been every bit as excited by the latest Enigma codes as Hunter had predicted. Contacts from U-boats were extremely rare and the implication of their latest find was not wasted on the professor. His stock was rising. Hunter handed over the sheets of recently printed German with Joth's hurriedly scrawled translations and then his work was done and the familiar wave of disappointment and regret swept over him. To make matters worse, the professor had no fresh codes for him to work on. Hunter reflected as he left his study that he had become a victim of his own success. Now he would have to find a job. On that point Amy had made herself abundantly clear and if he was going to take a job which would satisfy himself in any way intellectually, he would probably have to approach her ex-boyfriend, Alec Bell.

He sat in his favourite spot in Fellows' Gardens, his back pushed up hard against a cherry tree. The rhododendrons and azaleas were in full flower and putting on an unashamedly impressive display of pinks and reds, each bidding to outdo its neighbour. Usually he came to the gardens with a crossword or to work on his laptop but today there was something more serious on his mind. Alec Bell had been his closest friend and rival throughout university. They had done everything together; got drunk together, studied together, holidayed together. They'd spent a glorious week wandering Tuscany's ancient hill top villages, eating pizza, drinking cheap, weak local red wine and talking maths. Always talking maths. Their families had become close too, with dinner parties and idle promises of shared holidays. And then there had been Amy.

When Hunter first met Amy she and Alec had been a couple. The three had hung out together, gone drinking and Amy had tried, much to Hunter's annoyance and confusion, to set him up with any number of friends. Then Alec's career had taken off and he had started spending more and more time out of the country, the university sending their latest prodigy to seminars around the world, initially to attend and network and then latterly as a lecturer in his own right. Amy and Alec were becoming ships that passed in the night, whilst she and Hunter were spending more and more time together. Then one evening they'd finally summoned up the courage to talk about their feelings for one another. The following morning they'd woken up in the same bed and everything had changed. Alec, in that way that he had, shrugged it off. He'd even seemed genuinely pleased for his friends. Hunter couldn't help feeling that perhaps Alec hadn't always been as devoted to Amy as he might have whilst halfway around the world on the lecture circuit and to assuage his guilt had pictured his friend conducting sordid little affairs in grubby foreign hotel rooms. Hunter was no fool. He knew that if things had been different, if Alec had been more attentive, more dependable, Amy would probably have stayed with him. Although he didn't doubt she loved him, in the back of his mind was the ever present notion that he was in some way inferior, second best, a poor substitute for his playboy, globetrotting rival and friend. But, for whatever reason, and for the timebeing at least, she had decided to stay with him.

When they graduated the university immediately offered Alec a job on its staff, making him one of the youngest lecturers in its history. Hunter attended some of his early talks, and grudgingly had to admit that his friend wasn't just a gifted mathematician, he was an engaging and charismatic speaker too. Alec's lectures, which had started rather modestly less than a year before were now eagerly anticipated events in the College diary, with students, particularly young female undergraduates, coming from far and wide to attend. In the meantime Hunter sat in his student digs working on his algorithm and his Enigma codes. And now Amy was asking, no insisting, that he go and beg Alec for a job. A job which he knew entailed being Alec's dogsbody. He grabbed at a tuft of grass and yanked it violently from the ground. He wasn't sure he could do that. He was damned if he was going to be Alec's flunky. He would rather get a job sweeping the roads.

Hunter had been sitting in the same spot for over an hour and yet he felt every bit as confused and conflicted as he had done on leaving the house. Dejectedly he gathered up his paper, its crossword disappointingly incomplete, and thrust it into his messenger bag. Maybe the bus ride home would clear his head, bring him some answers? And if that didn't help he would just have to sit down with Amy and talk it through. Perhaps if Joth would lend him some money he might even take her out for a romantic evening, something to eat and then maybe a film? The Picturehouse was showing Casablanca.

The bus stopped on the other side of a busy roundabout and Hunter walked the remaining three hundred yards along a row of terraced houses. He opened his front door and saw immediately the thin brown envelope, folded neatly in half to ease negotiations with their dangerously aggressive letter box. Even before he had had a chance to examine it Hunter was surprised by its very presence. The post didn't normally come until much later in the day. But then again there really was no particular pattern to the post these days. He swung the bag off his shoulder, bent down and picked up the envelope. No stamp or postmark. That explained the Royal Mail's involvement, or lack there of. Hand delivered, the fold leaving a creased ridge which ran the length of the carefully typed white rectangular sticker bearing his name.

Without thinking Hunter opened the self-adhesive strip and removed the envelope's contents. A single sheet of white A4 paper. He turned it over. Four rows of letters, fifty-one in total, each in upper case, each grouped together in a batch of four and separated from the next by a hyphen. Four groups on each row except the last one which contained only one short group of three. Clearly a code. He frowned. Aside from that the page was blank. Nothing to say where or who it had come from. He looked closely at the letters themselves. They had been typed in the centre of the page. He couldn't swear to it but the font appeared modern, Verdana or Helvetica. Either way certainly not from the nineteen-forties and certainly not the product of a typewriter but of a modern printer which meant a modern source, probably a computer or laptop, and probably a laser printer as the quality seemed good having none of the inconsistencies associated with inkjet printing. He turned it over several more times in an effort to glean any last piece of information. Perhaps it was a practical joke sent by someone at the university. Alec was the most obvious candidate. It was just the sort of thing he might do. Hunter briefly considered not bothering to decode it at all but that thought soon passed. Maybe the deliverer of the mysterious code was still in the neighbourhood? He didn't remember passing anyone as he'd walked from the bus stop, certainly no one he'd recognised. But then he supposed they could just as equally have left in the opposite direction. Amy was still at work, but maybe Joth had seen someone? Perhaps this was Joth's handiwork? Payback for Hunter's nocturnal escapade the other day. But that didn't sit quite right, it wasn't the South African's style.

What could he have been thinking? It would be from Professor Sinclair, that was the most obvious explanation. Freddie had probably been meaning to present him with it earlier, but had become so wrapped up in their latest triumph that he'd forgotten and so dropped it off in a hurry on his way home. Strange then that there were none of Sinclair's neatly handwritten comments in evidence. Usually anything he sent Hunter was covered with speculative notes and diligently penned queries. He should make certain he hadn't just missed him.

Still holding the page and its envelope Hunter walked back outside. There was a light spring shower and the road seemed almost completely empty. No children at play, no dogs being walked, no commuters returning from a busy day's employ, just a gentle breeze, a mist of rain and two cars; the beaten up old blue VW Polo that belonged to the guy across the street and an impressive looking metallic black BMW 6 series parked slightly further up the road under a tree. No sign of the professor or his car.

***

There had been a time when cameras possessed real character, real style, each with its own subtly distinctive shutter sound and feel. The Olympus had been quick and nimble, the Pentax heavy but reliable and the Hasselblad had sounded exactly as it was, expensive. But no longer. The Cannon EOS 550D was set to continuous shoot which meant it could rattle off nearly four predictably reliable frames a second. With a Tamron telephoto lens Scott Hunter's face filled the view finder as he craned his neck to look up and down Danforth Road. A rapid reposition and the Cannon fired off four more quick frames of Hunter's hand clutching the page of white A4. Satisfied, the owner of the camera switched it off and placed it next to him on the BMW's nappa leather passenger seat.

***

Hunter meticulously worked through every stage of his routine. Despite its lack of provenance he would treat this latest code as if it had originated from either the Imperial War Museum in South London or the museum at Bletchley Park. But from the outset the process proved to be a frustrating one. Normally he expected at least to see the date on which the message had been intercepted. That was always a sound indicator as to the model of machine which might have sent it. Then, and assuming the message was German in origin, he would look for specific keywords. Bletchley Park, Hunter knew, had been incredibly successful in breaking Ultra codes sent during the

North African Campaign simply by searching for words like sandstorm or desert. However, all of this additional intelligence had been withheld, even the professor's unrelenting handwriting was absent and so as he stared at the lines of code Hunter couldn't help but think just how difficult they might be to break. He was going to have to set his programme up with the broadest of possible parameters and do something he had never countenanced before and which did not sit well with him now. He was going to have to hope for the best.

That evening, and once Amy had returned from the office, Hunter cooked whilst she slipped out of her work clothes and took a shower. She joined him in the kitchen and they shared a glass of wine together as she told him about her day. Hunter stood next to the cooker, keeping one eye on an array of pots and pans as Amy unburdened herself of the day's office politics. He loved listening to her as, glass in hand, she ranted and raved about her co-workers in a fashion that was simultaneously cathartic for her whilst designed to make him laugh.

Before the meal was ready, unable to help himself any longer, he'd caught her in his arms, spinning her around, pushing her against the tiny kitchen table, kissing her urgently, and then Amy, ever the voice of reason had gently reminded him not to burn their meal.

Over dinner Hunter told her of his decision to see Alec and realising how hard it must have been for him Amy leant across the table and gently kissed him on the cheek. 'Thank you,' she said simply.

They ate in silence, before Amy continued, 'Any idea what the job entails?'

'Research assistant, I'd imagine?'

'Oh.'

They both knew what that could mean. Perhaps it would be different working for Alec, she said. Amy certainly hoped so for Hunter's sake, although deep down she suspected it might be considerably worse.

The meal over, the wine gone Hunter half-heartedly suggested they watch a film, but it was Amy who took his hand and lead him upstairs to bed.

The following morning Hunter checked his laptop. It seemed to have made little or no progress. He'd had a feeling that might be the case. He would either have to go back to square one or at least significantly modify the criteria he'd started with. Hunter wondered at the possibility the message had not been German after all. It could be Italian, or, God help him, Japanese. As Hunter sat staring intently at the screen Amy appeared and let him know she was off to work.

'Good luck today,' she said deftly applying a delicate line of eye shadow.

He looked up at her, every bit the business woman in her slim fitting charcoal suit, Hunter's vacant expression giving him away.

'Today Scott, you'll see Alec, today won't you? Oh Scotty, please tear yourself away from that bloody thing for the morning at least.'

'Let me just finish this. I'm so close, I'm sure of it.'

'For Christ's sake. I give up. I thought we discussed this last night?'

'We did and I will, just let me finish this first.'

'Okay then.'

'I thought I'd go into college later and see...' he let the sentence trail off. She knew he was going to see Professor Sinclair, he could tell simply by the look on her face. Hunter had never understood her antipathy towards him. They had talked about it once, briefly. She was generally such a good judge of character and when he'd pushed her she'd been unable to say exactly what it was about the Head of Classics that made her feel so uncomfortable. Amy, not usually a believer in woman's intuition, had used just such a phrase. A feeling, an impression, she'd added quickly. Hunter couldn't help regretting that two people so close to him didn't get along better. Sinclair was his friend, Amy his partner. He felt certain that if she gave him a chance Amy would find she had a lot in common with the man.

'Well, anyway, whilst I'm in I'll go to Alec's department and find out what his schedule's like. All right?'

Amy shook her head in mild frustration. 'See you later,' she said, 'and for Christ's sake don't spent all day on that wretched laptop, you'll go blind.' She smiled and kissed him lightly goodbye.

Hunter pored over the problem for the remainder of the morning before finally admitting defeat. He didn't like asking for assistance. The challenge was only ever diminished when you asked for help. But in this case he had to grudgingly admit he was completely baffled. He went into his Gmail account and pulled up the group marked *Enigma*. There were ten members, nine not including

40

himself. He could discount the professor as he suspected the code had probably originated from him in the first place and anyway he planned on seeing him later that afternoon. In an act of staggeringly transparent self-interest Sinclair had roped in one of the modern history professors. He'd done the same with a member of the language department too. Hunter discounted them both. In any case, if he was still getting nowhere he could simply go and pay them a visit that afternoon and take the code with him. That left half a dozen whose interest was sporadic at best. There were two German historians, Beck and Schumacher, who ran an Enigma association of their own in Frankfurt. They might have been able to help had there been any historical information to go on, but as it was Hunter thought there was little point in involving them. Peter Gracewell was a man who claimed to have worked at Bletchley Park during the war but had never contributed anything to Hunter's knowledge and was viewed as little more than a Walter Mitty character by Sinclair. Next was Steve Morgan of Fort Lauderdale, Florida whose emails were repeatedly returned by the postmaster and who Hunter took the opportunity to delete. Alec's name was on the list too, but he knew he had only joined as an act of solidarity and neither had the interest nor the time to be of any help. And that left Lazarus.

Lazarus had always been something of a mystery. Hunter couldn't actually say when he had joined their exclusive little group or what his background had been either, but when he'd been stumped in the past the biblical brother of Mary and Martha had proven both helpful and knowledgeable and consequently they had struck up a brief online friendship. Lazarus it was then.

Need help. See file.

Once he'd scanned and attached the mysterious code, off it went. Immediately Hunter felt both elated and disappointed. He hated having to admit defeat, or at least what he considered to be defeat, but he was also optimistic that Lazarus would come back with something. He glanced at the clock in the top righthand corner of the screen. 14:17. Shit. He needed to get into town quickly before Sinclair left for the day. He jammed everything into the messenger bag, shouted farewell to Joth over his shoulder and ran from the house to the bus stop.

Hunter wasn't confident that he would catch Professor Sinclair as he walked rapidly up the picture lined corridor. He wrapped on the heavy oak door and was relieved to hear the professor's voice call back.

'Hello. Who is it?

'Scott, Scott Hunter. Could you spare me a moment Professor?'

The door swung open on heavy hinges and Professor Sinclair's weary face peered back at him.

'Hello, Scott. Is my diary not up to date? I wasn't expecting a call from you this afternoon.'

'Sorry,' Hunter replied rather breathlessly.

'As you can see,' Sinclair continued gesturing behind him at a desolate looking girl in her early twenties, 'I am trying, all be it rather unsuccessfully, to impart some wisdom to this young lady.' The young lady in question flashed Hunter an embarrassed smile.

'Perhaps I should come back later?'

'That might be for the best, if you wouldn't mind?'

'I just wanted to ask you about this,' Hunter said fishing in his messenger bag for the envelope, 'but I suppose it can wait.'

'May I?' Professor Sinclair was looking at him quizzically.

'You dropped it off yesterday afternoon?' Hunter suggested.

'Professor Sinclair,' his student's voice trailed across the study, 'I do actually have to be going now, I can be out of your way in just a second.'

'Oh, very well then. In you come, Scott,' he said taking the envelope from him and withdrawing its contents, 'What appears to be the problem?' Sinclair let his glasses dangle distractedly from delicate fingers, their temple tips edging closer to his pursed mouth as he scrutinized the sheet of A4.

'Well, it is a bit low on information, you'd have to admit? I put the programme onto it last night but so far, nothing. I was wondering if you could give me any pointers, like when it was sent or even just where it came from?'

Sinclair was at the door, escorting his student out.

'I don't know how some of these young people manage it,' he said turning the sheet over in his hands, 'she's pleasant enough, but really.' He slid the sheet back into its envelope and returned it to Hunter.

'I'm sorry, Scott, I don't think I can help you.'

'But I thought you sent it?'

Sinclair shook his head. 'Not this one, Scott.'

'Well if you didn't send it, who did?'

43

'I really couldn't say. Someone at the university? I've no idea. And you believe it's beyond your... gadget, do you?' Sinclair continued with an academic sneer, never having particularly approved of Hunter's 21st century approach.

'At the moment it seems so, yes.'

'Perhaps it just shouldn't be broken then. Has that ever occurred to you?'

'What?' Hunter had never heard the professor give up quite so easily.

'Let sleeping dogs lie and all that. Come along Scott, we've talked often enough about some of the traffic that must have been sent. Perhaps this is one of those?' Hunter knew exactly what Professor Sinclair was referring to and he could also see that he was cautiously presenting him with a convenient way out if his algorithm was unable to break the message.

'Maybe you're right,' Hunter said. Amy at least would be delighted to hear he'd given up on the thing.

'But if you are determined to keep at it, perhaps you might considered a more academic approach? There are a few books I could recommend?'

Hunter couldn't help feeling he was being just a little patronized. He had quite a collection of books not just on Enigma and Bletchley Park but on the German Abwehr, the Kreigsmarine and even some technical books from the war that he'd tracked down online and bought from private collectors, grudgingly paying Joth to translate the relevant passages for him. Without them he would never have been able to write the algorithm.

'*Enigma* by Philip Rutherland?'

Hunter nodded. That had been a dry read he thought, even for a mathematician.

'And what about, oh damn it,' Sinclair said, trying to draw the information from his memory, '*The History of Cryptanalysis in the Second World War?*'

Hunter thought for a moment, visualising the crowded bookcases next to his bed. This was a book he was not familiar with.

'Can you remember who it's by?' he asked.

'Oh, so there is something you've not read,' the professor said with a hint of glee. 'Stevens... No Stevenson. You'll forgive me I am terrible with names, a symptom of my advancing years you see? But yes I believe that's it. Such and such Stevenson. I've a feeling there's a copy in the college library. Do you still have your card?'

Hunter fumbled in his trouser pocket for his wallet, withdrew his CAMCard and found his blue University of Cambridge Library card. Expired.

'My my, your life is full of challenges today, isn't it Scott?'

✳✳✳

Hunter ran his eyes over the shelves. Many of the books he recognised, having either borrowed them or bought them cheaply online. He quickly found Andrew Stevenson's *A History of Cryptanalysis in the Second World War* and turned to its index, running his finger down the list of now familiar names before flicking back to the appendices. This was often where the really useful information was to be found. Stevenson had included a thorough set of schematic diagrams showing the wirings for many of the different machines. He tucked the book under his arm and began looking for *Enigma* by Philip Rutherland. As factual books went Rutherland's was about as lacking in soft edges and humour as Hunter could imagine. He found it on the same shelf as the Stevenson, wedged beneath a carelessly replaced book lying horizontally along the top of the row. He eased the weighty tome from the shelf and gave it the most cursory of glances. Yes, it was the book he had at home. Yes, it could, as the professor had suggested, be useful. No, he would not be wading through it later. He went to return the dry companion to its prescribed slot. The horizontal book had slid down and across and now sat angled inconveniently in his path. Without examining it he took it from the shelf and replaced *A History of Cryptanalysis*. As a gesture of goodwill and for allowing him to use and abuse the university's library system Hunter thought the least he could do was replace the book he now held in his left hand to its rightful home. Turning it over he read down the spine; *Setting Europe Ablaze; Coding for the SOE* by George Wiseman. On the cover the now ubiquitous picture of an Enigma machine. Hunter had never seen this book before. He glanced at the back cover. A friendly gentleman returned his gaze. George Wiseman's hair was thick, wavy and grey and pushed back from his high forehead. A prominent Hasidic nose nestled beneath twinkling eyes. Hunter had never seen an author with a cigar and wearing a velvet tuxedo and black tie before. He flicked through the book until he reached a collection of glossily printed black and white photographs at its heart. There was U-559, the U-boat whose crew, after sixteen straight hours of depth charges, had abandoned their vessel without, crucially for the allied war effort, first destroying its Enigma key setting sheets for the entire fleet. Next a photograph of the eclectic front aspect of the manor house at Bletchley Park followed naturally by a picture of Alan Turing, a faraway look on the face of the man responsible for so much of the extraordinary work undertaken at Station X.

Hunter licked a finger and turned the page. Two men, both wearing suits and ties, the younger of the pair, possibly nineteen or twenty, sat at a table behind an encoding machine, a scarf carelessly draped around his neck. To his side an older gentleman sporting a Fedora, his hand on the younger man's shoulder. Hunter found the caption.

The author with his father, Bletchley Park c 1948?

That was good enough for him. There was something in that photograph which fascinated Hunter. He wasn't sure, perhaps it was simply the relationship between Wiseman senior and his son and the thought of them working together. A father working hand in hand with his offspring against a shared enemy. He felt sure he was going to enjoy this book even if it revealed nothing new about Enigma.

Hunter fished in his jacket pocket and found his wallet. A quick look revealed what he already knew, he had no money and his CAMBCard, which up until recently would have granted him access to all but a few books in the great university's library system, had lapsed and was now sadly out of date. He shoved the wallet back in his jacket and glanced towards the doors. Two great metal arches protected the libraries contents. Each book would have to be introduced to a magnetic scanner before he could proceed through those arches without setting off the most appalling alarm. Briefly Hunter thought about checking his card again, but that was fatuous, he'd seen it only seconds before. Expired. How to proceed? Amy's card would be similarly expired he assumed. He could go back to his digs and see if Joth would take the books out for him, but then he had a feeling that his chaotic flatmate's stock with the university was probably even lower than his own. He looked at the books he was holding. Reluctantly he conceded there was nothing for it but to put them back and return another day, take a lot of notes and hope that that would be enough. He moved towards the shelf. But if he did that several things could happen. Someone else might borrow Wiseman's book. It was certainly unlikely, but nevertheless possible. Worse still someone might use them to decode the latest page before he did. He allowed himself a gentle pat on the back. Once more, possible, but unlikely. Hunter wasn't prepared to risk it. He had no idea why but he felt the sooner he got to the bottom of this particular riddle the better. He opened his messenger bag.

'Excuse me. Excuse me!' Hunter strode confidently through the metal arches, a copy of Philip Rutherland's drearily earnest *Enigma* clutched academically across his chest. As the alarms blared he continued up the long thin corridor and away from the university's library until he felt a firm hand fall on his shoulder. He span round quickly and took in the pinched face of the man who stood before him. A little shorter than himself at about five foot ten and probably, Hunter guessed, about ten years older. He was almost certainly a failed graduate who had dropped out of academia and been found a cosy little job working in the library. That, Hunter surmised would have been about seven or eight years ago. Those intervening years had not been kind on the man. He was mouthing something and glowering at Hunter's book.

Hunter very slowly and quite deliberately removed his head phones.

'I'm sorry, what?'

'You haven't signed for that book. You *must* sign for your book.' He held out his hand and Hunter made a grovelling apology. 'That doesn't matter,' the man was saying 'If you'll let me have your card, please?'

Hunter knew this was probably where his hastily thrown together plan would fall to pieces. He made great play of padding down his jacket and trousers in search of the elusive card, as the man opposite him looked on, his patience obviously stretched. 'It's here somewhere I'm sure it is.' He smiled what he hoped would be a winning smile and prepared for his next deceit. As he took his wallet from his jacket, in an act of nervousness it slipped from his hands. The library's guardian retrieved it for him. 'I'm so sorry,' Hunter stammered, opening it up and examining its leather compartments. 'It's just that I have a feeling,' his fingers were on the plastic rectangle now, 'that this may have expired.' He withdrew the obsolete card, turned it in his hand and smiled ruefully back at the librarian before bowing his head in an admission of his guilt.

'I will take this,' the librarian held up his copy of *Enigma* 'and this,' he snatched the card from Hunter's hand. 'You can be certain I shall be writing to your faculty head.' He was about to return to his precious wards, but then remembering, faltered, and angrily shaking the card at Hunter to emphasis his case continued, 'The bag. What's in the bag? Let me see.'

Hunter was blown. There was no point in denying it. He let the shoulder bag slip to the floor, where he knelt in an act of specious supplication and undid its clasps. He drew back the flap to reveal Andrew Stevenson's *A History of Cryptanalysis in the Second World War* lying on top of that day's copy of the Cambridge Times.

'Oldest trick in the book. Fucking students.' Hunter handed it to him.

'I'm so sorry.'

'You can now expect a strongly worded letter, and, as far as I'm concerned, you're barred.' Clutching the two recovered articles he sanctimoniously strode back to the library. 'Fucking students.'

Hunter, shamefaced and defeated resolved to take the first bus home.

✳✳✳

On the top deck of the 11A, Hunter opened his precious messenger bag, removed the folded newspaper, smiling at its weight, and watched as George Wiseman's book slid out.

Once home he quickly skimmed Philip Rutherland's book, taking notes as he went. His laptop continued to process the many millions of permutations as he made minute adjustments based on his findings. Then Amy appeared with a fresh pot of tea. She tried to lure him away with a DVD of *Jean de Florette* but Hunter told her to start without him. He was almost finished and would come down soon and pick it up from wherever she had got to. She hated him when he said things like that.

Once he'd finished with the Rutherland book he turned his attention to George Wiseman's. He had already dipped into it on the bus home. The writing style reflected the photograph of the author on the back cover. It was light, witty, irreverent, sometimes contentious and often extremely funny. Hunter couldn't put it down. Amy, having watched *Jean de Florette* alone, decided she would go to bed. She stood in front of Hunter and slipped provocatively out of her work clothes and into a night shirt.

'Come to bed?'

'I'll be there in a minute,' he'd said absently, hardly looking up.

When midnight came he was still reading Wiseman's book. He'd carefully arranged an angle poise so as not to disturb the sleeping Amy. At a half past one he called it a night and slid into bed next to her. She hardly stirred.

***

The Winstanley Lecture Theatre is part of Trinity College's Blue Boar Court, seating a hundred and fifty students. Hunter arrived at half past twelve, just in time to hear the general hubbub of a lecture finishing. The sound of a hall full of students packing away, discussing the talk or making social arrangements for the evening threw him back twelve months and he felt a sudden pang of nostalgia. The doors crashed open and a stream of undergraduates began to pour out. They looked so young, Hunter thought, so full of hope and ambition. He'd been like that once. He waited for the hall to clear. At the front, on the stage tidying away his notes, Alec Bell, smartly casual in a pair of chinos and an open necked shirt, his long perfectly maintained fair hair glowing warmly under the theatre's lights. If Hunter hadn't known him quite so well he could easily have mistaken him for one of his own students. He raised a hand in greeting and started down the theatre's raked steps. Alec stuck out his hand and then pulled Hunter into a bear hug, slapping him affectionately on the back.

'Come to ask me for a job?'

Alec had done what he always did, he'd jumped in and said the unsayable. Taken the elephant in the room and put him centre stage with a band and an MC and all in a manner that had defused the situation rather than enflaming it.

'You bastard. Who told you?'

'Sinclair mentioned something the other day.'

Hunter nodded. It was hard to be angry with either of them, after all, they were only looking out for him.

Alec finished packing away his notes and they walked up the stairs and out of the theatre together.

'I'll be honest, I'm not sure I can do it, work for you I mean.'

'If things were different I'd feel the same.'

'What do you mean by that?'

'There's no way on God's earth I'd work for you, Scott. You're far too...'

'Far too what?'

'Oh, I don't know.'

They walked the rest of the way to the exit in silence.

'In any case, you don't really fit my profile.' Alec finally said holding a door open.

'I'm sorry, and what do you mean by that? Don't fit your profile, what bloody profile?'

As they reached the front steps Alec was struggling not to laugh.

'Don't patronize me, Alec,' Hunter continued, 'In what way do I not fit your profile?' His temper was rising. How dare he. Alec might have the position, the car and the playboy lifestyle, but they both knew that intellectually there wasn't a hair between them, it was simply that Hunter had chosen not to flagrantly promote himself or court publicity. 'I'd like to know exactly what it is someone else can offer you that I can't?'

'Well, I can think of a couple of things straight off.'

Hunter was better qualified for this job than anyone. What the hell was he suggesting? Perhaps he hadn't had the obvious success that Alec had, but he didn't like the implication that he wasn't up to being his bloody assistant. He was every bit the mathematician Alec was.

'Shall I tell you what I'm really looking for in a job applicant?' Alec teased.

'I wish you would.'

'What I'm really looking for is someone who's about five foot six, long legs, platinum blonde hair down to about here,' Alec drew a line just above his waist, 'possibly with a twin sister and most crucially of all a great big pair of...'

'Got it. Got it, thank you for that vivid picture. I take it that will all be appearing in the paper when you finally get around to advertising?' Hunter was laughing now too. Alec the wind-up merchant. Alec the joker, always playing for laughs. Hunter chided himself. He ought to have known. This was simply the way their relationship had always been. Alec would wind him up to just such a point and then there would be the pay off, the punchline and invariably Hunter had to concede, with Alec placing himself firmly at the butt of his own joke. 'I can't wait to meet her... and her sister.' Now the joking was out of the way, Alec showed his other side. The side few people, girlfriends, adoring students, or journalists, ever saw.

'You're sure you're not up for it? Could be fun?'

'No,' Hunter said firmly, 'particularly not now. I don't want to have to take you to court for sexual harassment for one thing.'

'There is always that, although I'm not sure you're my type,' Alec laughed. 'Question is, what are you going to do? You can't spend the rest of your life buggering around with sixty-year-old bits of German.'

'Don't.'

'There's no money in it for one.'

'I am painfully aware of that.'

'Ah,' Alec smiled. 'The gorgeous Amy on your case? How is she?'

'She's fine and yes she is on my case, a bit. The problem is she's paying the rent, the council tax and all the other damn bills and all I'm bringing in is what I get from the government.'

'Bloody scrounger.'

'I knew you'd understand.'

'So, if I can't interest you in some research work, what *are* you going to do? Do you want me to keep an ear to the ground?'

'Would you mind?'

'Course not. Come on I'll buy you lunch.'

Hunter shook his head. He wasn't going to be a charity case and this time Alec knew not to push him.

'How about a pint then? The Champion?'

They walked along King Street to The Champion of the Thames Pub. It had been a regular drinking haunt when they had first met at college. Alec had been on the verge of a rowing blue, whiling away many happy hours trying unsuccessfully to ingratiate his way into the boat. They ordered a couple of pints and found a table in a secluded corner.

'What are you up to then?' Alec inquired.

'Well, I am still buggering around trying to break sixty year-old-codes, as you so eloquently put it. Although just at the moment I've got a real sod of a one.' Hunter put his drink down and stared long and hard at the white frothing residue left by the beer. 'I half wondered if you'd had something to do with it?'

'Me?'

'One of your childish attempts at humour.'

Alec snorted derisively. 'Sorry to disappoint, although it does sound like it's got you all riled up, but I'm afraid, this time, it's got nothing to do with me.'

So that cleared that up.

'I've widened the parameters as much as I can, but so far...'

Alec looked up at mention of the program. Privately he would have conceded that he'd been more than a little jealous of Hunter's success. For once it had seemed his friend might steal the limelight from him. Almost more annoyingly, Hunter had shunned any publicity. To Alec it had all looked like such a wasted opportunity.

'You must let me have a copy of that one of these days, I'm intrigued to see how you've put it together.' By way of an answer Hunter took a long drink. 'It could have the makings of quite an interesting paper,' Alec continued.

Hunter had made a promise to himself never to let anyone see the algorithm. Christ, Alec had enough didn't he? The girls, the money, the academic adulation. He was smart enough, if he really wanted to, to write his own bloody algorithm instead of gallivanting off around the globe appearing on late night phone ins and screwing chamber maids. Hunter shook his head.

'No chance.'

'I see. First you turn down a job, then you turn down lunch and now you won't even let your oldest friend misappropriate your life's work. Charming. What's the big problem anyway?'

'Like I said, I'm not getting anywhere with it. Normally you'd expect a certain degree of background, dates, times, places, that sort of thing.'

'And you didn't get any of those this time?'

'No, not a one.'

'That's a bit odd isn't it?'

'Sinclair's treating the whole thing like it's some sort of vindication that history works better than science. You can imagine the sort of thing?' Alec nodded 'You're much better off with a dusty old reference book and a slide rule. I don't hold with all this new-fangled electricity lark. Low-down. Bad juju.' Alec laughed at Hunter's impersonation. 'Mind you, he did put me onto *this*, in a roundabout sort of way.' Hunter fished about in his messenger bag and produced George Wiseman's book. 'Don't suppose you've read it?'

Alec gave him a look which said, in no uncertain terms, that of course he had not read it, at no stage in the future did he intend to read it, and not to be so bloody silly.

'You should, I think you'd enjoy it.'

'It's really not my kind of thing, Scott. I love the maths, but all that pseudo detective work and the Cold War spy crap,' he said pointing to the photograph of the book's author, 'It just doesn't do it for me. I mean, really, who does this guy think he is, Liberace?'

'Actually, I think he may hold the key.'

'Well?'

'Well, I rang his publishers first thing this morning to see if they would put me in touch with him, but they weren't playing ball. Apparently, they don't just hand out addresses to any old Tom, Dick or Harry.'

'Do you mind?'

Alec took the book from Hunter and went to the bar to order two more pints. When he returned it was wedged precariously under his chin. He handed Hunter his drink.

'If I can get this old goat's phone number for you will you let me have a look at the algorithm?'

Hunter took a sip of his second pint. It was a calculated risk, but the odds were stacked in his favour. Alec would never get the number. He'd already tried and failed and there was no reason to believe his friend would fare any better. After two more pints he agreed.

Alec took an iPhone from his pocket and placed Hunter's book on the table in front of him. He opened the Safari app and went online. Seconds later he had the phone number of the book's publishers and the phone was asking him if he would like to make a call. He brushed his thumb across the screen, put the mobile to his ear and shot Hunter a confident smile.

'Oh hello,' he began, 'who am I speaking with? Marta? Jak się masz Marta, nazywam sie Alec. Where are you from? No I'm afraid I don't know Poznan. I was in Warsaw last year though. Beautiful city.' Alec screwed up his face at the lie. 'Listen I'm George's editor. George Wiseman, daft old coot, wears a bow tie, partial to a cigar.'

Hunter shook his head.

'You don't know him? No? No reason why you should, I suppose. Anyway, listen I'm having lunch with a client and I really need to get his number but I've left my sodding contacts book in my other jacket. Would you mind?' Hunter looked at his friend in disbelief as they waited for the temp on the other end of the line. 'That is so kind of you Marta, would you just give me a second while I find a pen.' Hunter was horrified. He could see his beloved algorithm slipping from his grasp before his very eyes. Alec was gesturing frantically at him and so reluctantly he dug into the bottom of the shoulder bag and produced an old biro. 'Right, fire away,' Alec said, rubbing it in as he scribbled down the figures. 'Thank you so very much Marta, Do widzenia.'

And there, on the bar-mat in front of Hunter was George Wiseman's London telephone number.

'Since when do you speak Polish? You've never been to Poland in your life.'

'Since I started teaching a naughty little undergrad called Jolanta,' Alec said with a knowing grin. 'Algorithm please?'

* * *

Hunter waited until he was home to phone the number Alec had obtained for him. He settled himself at his desk, a notepad by his elbow and rehearsed what he might say. For his call to go unanswered once or twice Hunter could accept, but after the fifth or sixth attempt he was grudgingly starting to admit that either the number the Polish girl had given them was incorrect, possibly intentionally, or Mr George Wiseman simply did not wish to be contacted. He filled a page of his notepad with doodles. This would be the last time he would try before exploring other avenues, although at present he had no idea what those other avenues might be. He pressed the handset's redial button.

'Hullo.'

'Hello, I was wondering if I might speak to a Mr Wiseman?'

The man on the other end of the line took his time. Hunter heard him struggle to clear his throat.

'Who is this?' he asked, his once sonorous baritone now heavy with the suspicion of old age. 'Who is this? Did I ask you to call?' Suspicion now replaced by anxiety. 'Is this a cold call? Who is this?'

'Am I speaking to Mr Wiseman? Mr George Wiseman, the author?' Another lengthy silence, a silence in which Hunter knew that the man on the other end of the line was indeed George Wiseman and that he now had his full attention, the trick would be to keep him on the line.

'Yes. Yes it is,' Wiseman replied cautiously, his voice subtly softening. 'How did you get this number? This is a private telephone number.'

'Your publishers gave it to me.'

'Did they indeed? Well, they had no bloody right to. I've half a mind...' Hunter could tell that there was a danger Wiseman was about to replace the phone firmly in its cradle. He cut in quickly.

'Could I talk to you about your book, Mr Wiseman?'

'Good Lord, well I suppose so. Which one would you like to talk about?'

'Setting Europe Ablaze?'

'Now where on earth did you uncover a copy of that unholy relic?'

'Trinity College library.'

'Well then, how may I help you, young man?' Wiseman was positively chatty now so Hunter decided it was time to see just how amenable the author really was.

'The thing is, and I know this is a terrible imposition, but I wondered if I might be able to come and talk to you in person?'

Silence.

'Mr Wiseman?'

More silence. Hunter began to worry he had pushed too soon. But now with nothing to lose it was better to press on.

'I have something I should very much like to show you. It's a bit of a long story and I really can't explain it over the phone.'

'Go on.'

'So if I could meet you in person, well, that would be most helpful.'

'I do not receive visitors, as a rule.'

Hunter's heart sank. And just when he'd thought he'd been getting somewhere.

'I'd particularly like to talk to you about Enigma.'

'Ah, yes. A fascinating piece of equipment. The Poles were the first to have any success with it you know?'

Hunter did know.

'Różycki, Zygalski and...' Wiseman left the sentence dangling invitingly, like a fly before a trout. This was it. This was Hunter's way in. The old man was testing him, his knowledge of Enigma. Not much of a test admittedly but the implication was clear; No time wasters.

'Rejewski. They were mathematicians. They broke Enigma in the December of 1932.' Hunter replied trying to hide the triumph in his voice.

Wiseman's silence was only broken by an unproductive wet cough.

'Can you be in London tomorrow?'

'Certainly.' Even as he was agreeing Hunter was frantically trying to recall what his plans were for the following day, or if in fact he had any plans at all. Amy would understand, probably.

'24 Lansdowne Terrace, 12 o'clock. Use the third buzzer down. I should take Gloucester Road tube if I were you, it's the nearest. And please don't be late. I abhor tardiness.'

'Thank you Mr Wiseman, I shall see you tomorrow and try my utmost not to keep you waiting.'

'Be sure you do. By the way young man,' Wiseman rumbled on, 'you never did tell me your name.'

'Hunter. Scott Hunter.'

'Is it? Well Mr Hunter I shall see you tomorrow at 12 o'clock,' and with that the line went dead.

Hunter was admiring Alec's beer-mat and wondering about train times when Amy entered.

'Who was that on the phone?'

He hesitated. How much should he tell her?

'I've got to go to London. Tomorrow.'

'Job?' She looked at him hopefully. Hunter was so desperate not to disappoint her.

'Yes, could be. An interview at any rate.' That was a half truth.

'Oh Scotty! That's great.'

'Thanks. You couldn't lend me some money could you?'

Amy rushed to find her purse and a fresh twenty pound note, leaving Hunter to feel like the lowest kind of con-man. If Wiseman could put him on the right track with this code he vowed he'd pay Amy back the money and take her out somewhere special, perhaps even give the coding a rest for a while and start seriously looking for a job. He greedily took the note from her.

'I'm so proud of you.'

She pulled him to her and kissed him as she struggled to take off her work jacket. Hunter's hands slid around her slim waist. He dragged her down onto the bed.

***

Sir John Alperton sat in The Nightingale just off Berkely Square. He loved the gastro-pub. He might be a Knight of the Realm and have been to university with half the cabinet, but none of that stopped him from being extremely fond of The Nightingale's steak and kidney pies. The kidneys were never over cooked and the crust was made from suet which soaked up the juices and melted in the mouth. That was why she'd suggested they meet there. She was going to try and squeeze him for some juicy titbit of information. Patricia bloody Hedley-King, god what an appalling specimen. He knew what she was up to. She was trying to soften him up, that was why she'd suggested The Nightingale. It was where she always took him for dinner when there were dark storm clouds gathering. Sir John prepared himself for bad news. She was playing all her winners early tonight though he noted looking at his watch. She'd kept him waiting nearly half an hour so far, bloody civil servant.

He ran a hand down his tie. Japanese silk. A little present to himself. Another glance at his watch. All part of her silly little power game of course. It hadn't been entirely bad though he conceded pouring himself a glass of claret. The pub also had a fantastic wine merchants. He'd ordered a Châteauneuf-du-Pape. A tired, old fashioned grenache still trading on past glories, which, being largely out of step with the rest of the wine growing world, reflected his mood rather pleasingly and of course The Home Office would pick up the tab. As he raised his wrist to check the time once more there was a commotion by the door separating the main pub from the rather exclusive dining area at the rear and then in she strode. Christ what a state. The product of some insufferable girl's school where they bred these witches, he supposed. Her hair was all over the place and she seemed to be wearing some sort of strange woollen garment covered in tassels and beads. Not the faintest attempt at any sense of style. She looked like a bloody lesbian and in keeping with her kind, just dressed however she damn well pleased. They might well both have been pushing sixty, but even after all that time working side-by-side, Sir John could only think of one shared interest. He prepared himself for the worst.

'John, so sorry to keep you waiting,' Hedley-King offered up a limp hand. Yes, I bet you are he thought, noting her over familiarity.

'Not at all dear lady, not at all. How are you?'

'Couldn't get an arsing cab.'

Hedley-King was scraping a chair noisily towards the table before any of the waiters could offer her assistance, whilst simultaneously gesturing for some service.

'I'm fine, really I'm fine. Unfortunately the same can't be said for the fucking minister who is currently down the road having any number of shit fits. I won't bore you with the details, I'm sure you can imagine. Usual bloody carry on. This latest batch John, really they are so *fucking* hopeless, I think they may be even worse than the previous lot.' There at least was one thing upon which they could agree. She instinctively reached into her handbag and without thought withdrew a packet of cigarettes and a cheap plastic lighter. Sir John looked wistfully at the tableaux taking shape before him as the recently arrived waiter continued to hover dejectedly by her shoulder. The years of guilt, associated and real, all summed up by one simple cigarette.

'So,' she teased it nearer her pursed lips, 'does he know?'

Alperton stared at her. What kind of damn fool question was that? Does he know, does he know *what*? In their line of business information was everything. Nobody really knew anything, *that* was very much the point. A warning shot across the old girl's bows to shut her up.

'He's working it out, yes.'

'With a little help from your good self, no doubt?'

Sir John contemplated the elegant stalk of his wine glass, turning it slowly in his fingers, pleased to see that not quite everything had become boorish and coarse.

'Turkey?'

Alperton snorted and turned his attention to the menu. The pies here really were exceptional.

'Turkey? *Istanbul?*' Hedley-King asked again more forcefully. 'Does he know?'

'I said he was bright, not a fucking clairvoyant.'

'Right. Well there's something I suppose.'

'I had a feeling you might feel like that.'

The cigarette brushed Hedley-King's lips. She seemed about to answer, then picked up the lighter which lay next to her side plate and scraped the spark wheel redundantly over its flint. 'How dare you,' she hissed.

'Bit of a public place to be washing one's dirty laundry wouldn't you say, old thing?'

Alperton straightened his serviette and sipped at his wine. 'Try the steak and kidney pie, it really is rather excellent.'

'I don't eat meat, as I'm sure you damn well know.'

Jesus, whatever next. No wonder her career had ended up as it had.

'All right John, I'll keep it simple for you,' she continued, all smarm and artifice forsaken.

'Oh, would you? How super,' Alperton replied, rising to the cause. This was his preserve and he was damned if he'd be pushed around by a civil servant, even if it were the redoubtable Patricia Hedley-King. 'Will you try the asparagus I wonder, or perhaps the crayfish? How are you about crayfish? Do they count?'

'Will he be ready?'

The waiter at her shoulder, unable to hold his countenance another moment, lent forward. 'I'm sorry madam,' he said sheepishly shaking his head at the cigarette. Sir John gave her a look which he hoped expressed his filial camaraderie and not his utter contempt and watched as she rolled her thumb over the sparkwheel once more.

'What do I have to do to get a fucking drink in this place?' she hissed, taking in a lung full of smoke. John Alperton was really growing to hate these meetings.

✳✳✳

Hunter settled back into his seat on the 9:18 from Cambridge to Liverpool Street. All being well he ought to have just enough time to get around the Circle Line to Gloucester Road and perhaps even grab a cup of tea before turning up to meet George Wiseman at midday. That morning he'd woken early to find an email from Lazarus. He was unable to help and so now the old man was looking like his only real hope.

The train would take an hour and a half. Hunter would use the time to finish the last few chapters of *Setting Europe Ablaze* and contemplate what lay ahead. As the Cambridgeshire countryside flashed by he took a propelling pencil from his jacket pocket and with a degree of satisfaction, underlined a spelling mistake in George Wiseman's book.

✳ ✳ ✳

David took the dusty cardboard box downstairs and into the living room. At one end of the room his high end stereo system, a seldom watched television and DVD player. The other corner was where he kept his geriatric computer. At the far end of the lounge, taking up the majority of the room, a large dining table. It hadn't always been a dining table. David had bought it at auction ten years ago. It had come from one of the many huge snooker halls of the North West. A nine-foot Riley billiard table made in oak with a slate bed and still with its original cushions, their perished rubber now hard and brittle. Whenever David used the table he was reminded of how it had come into his possession, a consequence of the long-abandoned halls, the table sold off without it ever being played on. Now, with its thick round legs and the right chairs, it made the perfect dining table. David didn't entertain anymore.

He had paid to have four sturdy interlocking oak panels made which protected the slate bed and created the dining space. These wore a gigantic spread of green baize. The unopened bills and unanswered letters which had littered the table, along with a glass ashtray which David hadn't used for that purpose in years, had all been piled up and removed. Then he'd covered the baize in old newspapers and laid out the tools he thought he might need in neat, vertical rows, much as a surgeon might. Between the tools he'd left a space at the centre of the table. He placed the box carefully on the paper. Everything was ready. Well, not quite everything. *He* was not ready. He was not yet ready to open it, this dusty old box which had languished in his attic for the last 18 years, since he had moved out of London to Hertfordshire and the countryside, not yet ready to confront its contents which had quietly haunted him for all of that time. He went to the kitchen, considered splashing his face with cold water but instead returned with a fresh cup of strong, black coffee.

Slowly he peeled back the cracked, yellowing Sellotape from the box and screwed it into a crispy ball. A quick slug of coffee to steady the nerves and then, finding fresh resolve, he folded back the cardboard and withdrew the contents in one determined, fluid motion. He placed the dusty black plastic bag at the centre of the table, unwound the faded grey masking tape holding it all together and peered inside. Then he sank quietly into his chair and began to cry.

3

Hunter emerged from the underground on Gloucester Road and into the stifling mugginess of Central London in the grip of a spring heatwave. Liverpool Street Station had reminded him just how many people there were in the nation's capital and then there had been the tube journey which had proven both uncomfortable and claustrophobic.

With little time to spare he dived into a coffee shop, and consulted his A to Z. He should head along Queen's Gate, past the Natural History Museum and on and up towards The Albert Hall. Consulates and foreign embassies appeared around every corner. Bumptious doormen in green and gold top hats posed for photos with Japanese tourists outside swanky four storey hotels, their window boxes trailing petunias and gasping fuchsias. Cambridge's omnipresent bicycles replaced by Mercedes 4x4s, Porsches and Jaguars, and all of them sporting the most recent plates.

The further he walked from the tube and the Cromwell Road the more Hunter noticed the subtle changes in the people around him. There were fewer of the vaping hipsters and tourists who flocked to Harrods and the museums and more students, presumably attending Imperial College, but others carrying violins or strangely shaped cases containing French horns or trumpets. They could have been performing at The Albert Hall, but judging by their age were probably studying at the Royal College of Music directly opposite. Hunter followed a girl as she wheeled a cello along the busy pavement. Perhaps she was on her way to practise some Bach or rehearse a Beethoven quartet, maybe perform the Brahms Double to a packed concert hall. He'd heard a recording of that once at the professor's. To Hunter it had sounded as though the soloists had never met before, but then Sinclair had assured him they were two of the world's finest. At a zebra crossing the girl manhandled her instrument over the road and the debate was settled.

Hunter consulted his A to Z for what he hoped would be the last time, checked the clock on his phone and turned into Lansdowne Terrace, Royal Borough of Kensington and Chelsea, W8, a prepossessing, narrow, tree lined row barely wide enough for a car. Rich, verdant branches overhung the road, the white washed walls of the flats and town houses starkly offsetting their dark green foliage. Hunter assumed that, behind their wrought iron security doors and close circuit televisions, many of the houses did not have access to a garden, and so had instead chosen to display lines of beautifully maintained planters with magnolias, hydrangeas and even a surprisingly healthy olive tree. Then he reached a house which must have had a roof garden and was drenched in sweet smelling wisteria. Along the pavement freshly painted black bollards and presiding over the whole spectacle a succession of the most extraordinarily ornate chimney pots Hunter had ever seen, each one a unique work of art and each worthy of its own place in the V&A just a few streets away. Nearest the main road, on its corner and at one end of a short parade of pet salons, extravagant florists and beauty parlours, a small and exclusive looking patisserie and café with a selection of Kensington's most exclusive ladies doing lunch and smoking long and exclusive cigarettes, whilst successful men with delicate dogs confidently clip-clopped past them on their way to rule the world. To Hunter the women might all have been opera singers or baronesses, by their feet expensive paper bags containing expensive little treats. None of this of course was helping him feel any more at ease. He was acutely aware of his student clothing and his almost total lack of local knowledge. He pulled his jacket over his New Order t-shirt and tried to calm the butterflies in his stomach and appease the encroaching waves of nausea brought on by a mixture of social anxiety, an absence of any proper breakfast and the unpleasant tea he had forced down at Gloucester Road.

Added to which Hunter realised all too late that finding number 24 was not going to be quite as straight forward as he had initially assumed. There seemed to be no rhyme or reason to any of the house numbers and he quickly resigned himself to looking at each property in turn, whilst keeping one eye trained on his phone as it counted down to midday.

At three minutes past twelve he found it. He took the dozen steps up to the entry buzzers two at a time before scanning down the list of opulent names. The third buzzer, that was what Wiseman had said. But there was no name in the polished brass fitting. No strip of paper, no card. He checked again. This was number 24 and that was the third buzzer down, but then Wiseman had never said his name would be up there in flashing lights. Consistent Hunter supposed, with a man who did not approve of a publisher giving out his telephone number. He pressed the button. As he waited and praying the old man would still see him, Hunter looked back down the elegant row towards the café. There certainly was some money around here. There was the latest Bentley, behind that an Audi and a brand new Daimler and just a little further along, partially obscured by a tree, a blacked out BMW 6 series. Suddenly the curtains at the window next to him moved to one side and then just as quickly fell back into place.

'You're late,' Wiseman grumbled over the intercom and then the grating electronic buzz sounded as the security door opened. Hunter moved inside and along a short, tiled corridor to a smartly painted front door with an elegant brass knocker and the discreetest of matching brass nameplates.

The George Wiseman that greeted him had aged considerably since the publicity photograph for his book jacket had been taken. This Wiseman wore a hearing aid discreetly tucked behind his ear and Hunter thought he had probably shrunk too, although it was impossible to say of course. He had lost none of his style though, that was for sure. Hunter imagined he didn't receive too many guests these days and had made a special effort for the occasion. He wore a rich, dark blue velvet jacket and open necked shirt. Hunter briefly caught sight of a gaudy gold wristwatch and a pair of ostentatious cufflinks, a red silk handkerchief providing his top pocket with a spray of colour.

'Good afternoon Mr Hunter, won't you please come in?'

Hunter smiled a polite hello as Wiseman pushed past him, stepping quickly into the shared vestibule at the front of the building to check that the exterior security door had closed firmly behind his guest.

The flat opened out into a small yet tastefully decorated entry hall. Hunter saw the old man had a passion for cricket; on a coat stand a cotton sunhat from Lord's and below it a cricket bat covered with the faint red spots of years of use. There were umbrellas and walking sticks and rather incongruously a baseball mit. Beside the front door, watching over the space, hung a large and imposing oil of a strikingly beautiful woman in furs. To Hunter's untrained eye it looked like a portrait of the highest quality. He could see two doors at the far end of the hall, presumably bedrooms, a kitchen or bathroom and each exhibiting the destruction of a seemingly absent cat. The old boy scurried past him, indicating a door to Hunter's left, the sitting room and the room from which Wiseman had inspected him just a moment before. Pushed to one side a baby grand piano, no longer a musical instrument but now a piece of furniture, its lid home to dozens of black and white photographs. There were many portraits of a young woman, probably Wiseman's wife, and many of the author himself, one of him laughing on a yacht, another in black tie, cigar in hand, a third of him standing beaming proudly next to a man Hunter half recognised in cricketing whites and a baggy cap. Behind the piano rose an elegant mahogany bookcase which Hunter was eager to examine. In the bay window a gate legged table, its leaves folded away, a 1960s Olivetti typewriter perched at one end. Once it had clearly been heavily used but seemed neglected and lonely now, its best days behind it, its purpose, like the baby grand's, purely decorative. To the left of the Olivetti another smaller table and a telephone.

Along one wall stretched a luxuriant black leather Chesterfield and facing it the central feature of the room, an impressive fireplace which could easily have heated the entire flat had it been lit, but was instead home to a fine collection of pine cones. Down each side of the fireplace, painted Victorian tiles in a dark red and above, a long, broad mantel piece brimming with yet more photographs. The majority of these seemed to be colour, of children awkwardly posed in school uniforms or at play. Grandchildren, Hunter supposed.

'Please.' Wiseman said gesturing towards a well-worn leather armchair angled at the empty fire. Hunter sat obediently. 'Now may I get you something to drink?'

Hunter thanked him and Wiseman turned and opened a cabinet to one side of the piano. He'd been hoping the old man would leave and go to the kitchen, providing him with an opportunity to examine the many collections of photographs and books, but instead, before Hunter could change his mind, Wiseman was bearing down on him with a glass of golden brown liquid and a small jug of water. Whisky at midday, on an empty stomach?

'Thank you,' he stammered.

'Water?'

'Yes. Plenty. Thank you.'

Wiseman regarded him disappointedly before splashing some water into Hunter's glass and taking some for himself in an act of grudging solidarity. Clearly this was not how he thought whisky should be taken. With a little effort he pulled up a chair.

'Used to drink whisky with a chap in Bursa,' Wiseman said smiling at the recollection, 'He took water too. Poured such a miserly measure we used to call it a mirage. Let's go round to Jerry's for a mirage, we'd say. Funny chap. Dead now, of course.' He looked up and away and Hunter wondered if he might not have had a wasted journey.

'So, how may I help you? It has been a long time since I received such an enigmatic request.' He smiled obsequiously, acknowledging the pun. 'I take it my publishers were unable to assist you?' Rather than answer that particular question Hunter produced his copy of the book. 'Well well, may I?'

The author took it from him, slipped on a pair of reading glasses which had been dangling carelessly around his neck, and with a look of unabashed pride began examining his work, nodding at it approvingly. Before Hunter could stop him the old man had taken a fountain pen from his jacket pocket, extravagantly signing his name on the inside cover, seemingly oblivious to the sticker on the facing page clearly stating it was the property of Trinity College Library. Then having diligently shaken the ink dry, he handed the book back.

'Would you mind if I ask you a few questions about Enigma?'

'Certainly,' Wiseman replied.

Hunter took an apologetic sip of his whisky. Surely to God nobody with an ounce of self respect could put this stuff willingly in their bodies, especially before lunch. The slightly sickly smell as the single malt caught at the back of his throat. He returned the glass to its table and tried to hide his feelings.

'You worked on it during the war?'

Wiseman's brow furrowed and he fiddled peevishly with his hearing aid.

'After the war. I take it you have read my book, Mr Hunter?'

'I'm sorry. After the war.'

'My father worked for the SOE during the war and then latterly at Bletchley Park. He must have seen in me some aptitude for the work and so I briefly assisted him. We may have had to stretch the truth a little with regards to my age, you understand?' Wiseman added with a mischievous grin.

'I can't remember, does your book ever actually say what work your father did?'

'No. That would be because the nature of my father's work was, like so much at Bletchley, rather sensitive, do you see? Few are aware, for instance, that after the war, with Churchill still determined Bletchley be kept under wraps, many of the technologies captured from the Germans were passed on to our friends in the colonies.'

'Passed on?'

'Yes.'

'Which technologies?'

Wiseman produced a leather case and, stifling a wet cough, lit an impressive cigar before addressing Hunter through a thick fug of smoke.

'Enigma, and the like.'

'Really?' Hunter could scarcely believe what he was hearing. 'Are you telling me the British government sold German Enigma machines to the Commonwealth?'

'I wouldn't have said sold exactly, but yes, that's the gist of it.'

Hunter gave a shocked laugh and reached for his glass.

That was good, Wiseman thought, watching the youngster persevering with his drink. Laughter was a good sign. It had been a deliberately naughty little tale, designed to be just grubby enough to keep the young pup happy. A cheeky reverse sweep, showy and eye-catching yet, ultimately inconsequential and certainly not to be repeated.

'And was it passed on as a secure network?'

'Mr Hunter,' Wiseman stopped to suppress another cough, 'secure is such a relative term, wouldn't you say?'

'No. Not particularly. Certainly not when it comes to something as sensitive as Enigma. Were the respective countries made aware that it had been broken?'

Wiseman swirled the spirit around his glass and watched it cling to the sides.

'You know, I'm not sure they were. Enigma was unbreakable, as far as the colonies were concerned at least.'

'Giving our government the ability to listen in on their secure chatter.'

'That would be the logical conclusion, I suppose. A little Trojan horse, if you like,' Wiseman said chuckling to himself.

'That's a bit unscrupulous isn't it?'

'Is it? I'd never really thought of it like that.'

'And your father?'

They listened as Wiseman's cigar hissed and crackled before the old man replied.

'My father?'

'Was that what he was involved in? Systematically eavesdropping on our allies?'

Wiseman tapped his Montecristo firmly on the ashtray by his side and watched contentedly as the cigar's ashen tip fell off.

'What did you say it was you are studying at Cambridge?'

'Mathematics.'

'Oh dear, I am sorry.'

Hunter chose to ignore the slight and pressed on.

'And I'm not studying actually, I graduated last year.'

'Good Lord, you don't look old enough. Well, I'm sure your parents must be extremely proud.'

He hadn't travelled all that way to talk about his parents and so there settled an uncomfortable silence between the two men. Wiseman smoked whilst Hunter wondered how best to salvage the situation. The old man took another sip from his tumbler.

'Truly, I'm sorry,' he said sensing Hunter's discomfort, 'that really was none of my business. Now, you have something you wish to show me?'

Hunter reached into his shoulder bag and produced the sheet of code, looking at it one last time before conceding defeat, willing the letters to magically spring from the page and rearrange themselves there and then. But when they didn't, he handed it to George Wiseman. The old man retrieved his reading glasses before carefully balancing his cigar on the heavy crystal ashtray at his elbow.

'My doctors keep telling me I'm to pack it in,' he said distractedly, not looking at the sheet of code. 'They say if I don't I'll have to have some sort of operation,' he continued theatrically drawing a line down his chest from his throat to his stomach. 'That sort of thing. Horrid little buggers, doctors, don't you think? Well they aren't getting their hands on me, I can tell you. And anyway, I think, once you get to my age, you're entitled to stop listening to doctors all together, don't you?'

Hunter said that he had to agree and began moving uneasily in his chair as the old man slowly inspected the page, his tired, watery eyes flicking up from time to time to study him.

'And where did you say you came by this?' he finally asked, retrieving his cigar.

'I didn't.'

'I see. Well, thanks for the trip down memory lane, but I'm not sure how I can be of any use to you whatsoever. It's a quatsch, you see?'

'I beg your pardon?'

'It's rubbish. Gibberish.'

There was something in the old man's tone. Hunter knew a brush off when he heard one, and he didn't like being lied to. There was more here, something the old man knew but wouldn't share.

'I don't believe so,' he suggested tentatively.

'You don't believe so? I see. And what may I ask, makes you say that?'

'Well, erm. I mean, nothing specific I suppose its just...' It crossed Hunter's mind that perhaps it had all been one of Alec's pathetic attempts at humour after all. Maybe he was wasting everyone's time whilst Alec sat in a pub somewhere howling with laughter at his gullibility?

79

'I mean, I suppose it could all be…' Hunter shook his head. He'd been a fool and an idiot. He'd wasted twenty pounds of Amy's money which he would struggle to pay her back, not to mention all the lies he had told.

'All right then,' Wiseman cut in abruptly, 'have you considered Playfair?'

Now Hunter was shocked. Was the old man being deliberately rude, trying to provoke him? Double Playfair had been one of Germany's most rudimentary codes and even suggesting such a thing to him was insulting.

'It's a single. There's no depth,' Hunter continued, trying to encourage Wiseman to take him a little more seriously.

'I can see that, young man.'

Then why did you suggest Playfair?

'And there's no crib either.'

'In which case, Scott, as I think I said, I fail to see how I can assist you.'

Wiseman puffed at his cigar, closing his eyes to savour the taste as he thought.

'Have you checked for numbers?'

Hunter nodded. It had been the first thing he had done.

'Punctuation?'

'I don't think there is any.'

'That would be highly unusual, you'd have to agree?'

Again Hunter nodded. They'd explored every possibility. Wiseman had been his last hope but the author had been unable or unwilling to shed any fresh light on the code, if indeed it was a code and not some cruel practical joke. There simply wasn't enough to go on. He regrettably had to acknowledge that the old boy was probably right. It was perhaps time to call it a day, return to Cambridge, make up something plausible to tell Amy and try and forget about the whole strange business.

'You never did tell me how this came to be in your possession?'

'It was left me.'

'Left you? Bequeathed to you in a will, was it?'

'No. Left on my door matt. Shoved through the letter box.'

'By whom?'

'I don't know.'

'Why you then?'

'I don't know that either. I break codes. It's what I do. I'm in a club you see, we try to crack old Enigma codes… for fun.'

'For fun! Dear God, boy.' The old man's face hardened and he angrily stubbed at his cigar before thrusting the code back at Hunter. 'I can assure you this is no game. People lost their lives over such things. Fun indeed.'

'I'm sorry.' Hunter said, with the meeting now in danger of becoming more of a disaster than he could ever have predicted. 'I chose my words poorly. As a mathematician there is something both beautiful and elegant about Enigma. That's what fascinates me, the intellectual challenge.'

'That is very much the problem with you mathematicians, if you'll forgive me for saying. You lack empathy and imagination. Not everything in life can be boiled down to ones and zeros, as I'm afraid you will discover.'

Hunter certainly didn't need the lecture. He was painfully aware of life and its many complexities.

'And you still haven't told me who left you this?'

'That's because I don't know.'

'Why you then, why would they choose you?'

'I break codes. It's what I do.'

'No, that's not it. Anyone could have broken this.'

'I'm not sure *anyone* could have,' Hunter said, struggling to disguise the dent to his pride.

Wiseman relit his cigar and fiddled with his hearing aid some more. 'Perhaps,' he said, the corners of his mouth threatening to curl into a conciliatory smile. And then, just as quickly the moment passed.

'I can't help you I'm afraid. It appears your journey may have been a wasted one.' With a little difficulty the old man rose from his chair to freshen his drink. 'This,' he continued, pointing to the sheet of paper in Hunter's hand, 'is a dead duck. Has it ever occurred to you that perhaps it should just be left well alone?' Wiseman stared at him, the frustrated teacher and the obdurate child.

'That's exactly what Sinclair said. Perhaps you're right?' Hunter threw back the last of his scotch and seeing the old man make no effort to refill his glass, assumed he had outstayed his welcome and that it was now time to do battle with London's over stretched transport system once more. But Wiseman's anger appeared to have evaporated.

'I beg your pardon?'

'Professor Sinclair, he kind of runs our club,' Hunter said, surrounding the word in silent and apologetic parentheses. 'He thought perhaps this one should be left alone too.'

'Did he now?' Wiseman massaged the arm of his chair. 'Professor Josef Sinclair?'

'Freddie Sinclair, Head of Classics.'

'My mistake.' Wiseman nodded to himself, 'Now I come to think of it, I couldn't swear Josef was a Cambridge man. That is just one of the many problems of advancing old age, I'm afraid.'

Hunter picked up his things and handed back his empty tumbler.

'I can heartily advise against it,' Wiseman continued, 'Old age, I mean.'

Hunter had turned towards the door and the hall and was already thinking apprehensively how he would return to Liverpool Street.

'Now, where do you think you are going? Sit, sit and let's begin again. You're missing something. What is it you're not telling me?'

Hunter let out a quiet sigh of exasperation. Really, where were they going with all this? But as much to put off sitting on a crowded tube train as anything he decided he would humour the old man. Slowly he related his routine to Wiseman on receiving a new code. He told him how he would log all the relevant information, adding that in this case there had been very little. He described the ring binder he used, right down to its colour and even mentioned the post it notes and where the folder was kept. He told the silent Wiseman as much about the algorithm as he thought he would understand and then just when Hunter believed he had unburdened himself entirely, right down to the last pointless little detail, Wiseman stirred.

'So please, Mr Hunter, tell me everything again, from the beginning and this time be more specific. Be careful not to omit a single detail.'

'You're kidding. I've just told you everything.'

Beneath their wrinkles, Wiseman's eyes hardened.

'My age, you understand? At my age it is sometimes necessary to repeat things, sometimes several times. Please indulge me, you returned to your digs. We shall continue from there. Then what did you do? You're forgetting something, intentionally or not.'

'There's nothing more to tell. Once I'd ascertained it was a code and checked to see I hadn't just missed the professor, I processed the information the way I always do. Like I just told you.'

'You saw this Professor Sinclair?'

'No, I left the house to make sure I hadn't just missed him.'

'Go on,' Wiseman urged.

'That's all. I stuck my head out to see if he was still around. He wasn't. That's it.'

'No. There's more. Who *did* you see?'

'No one. It was raining I think. There weren't even any cars on the road, just the one opposite and a black Beamer parked a few doors up.'

'Beamer?'

'BMW. Black. Looked brand new. Tinted windows, the whole thing.'

'There. Thank you, Scott. Now you have told me everything.'

The old man seemed oddly preoccupied, rubbing his thumb over his finger as if searching for something that had never been there. Hunter took this as his cue to leave. 'Thank you for the drink and your time Mr Wiseman, I think I'd better be going.'

'Of course, of course. Thank you for coming to see me. It's been years since anyone's expressed an interest in my writing,' he said cheerfully.

They were at the door now and Hunter turned to shake the old man's hand. Even though he didn't consider the meeting a success, and had found the irascible old boy somewhat temperamental and difficult to handle he couldn't deny having warmed to him.

'Thanks again. I'm sorry I hope I didn't upset you earlier.'

'No no, not at all. You must excuse me. Don't forget, young man, that when I was a little younger than yourself I actually saw the men responsible for breaking Enigma with my own eyes, I may even have met some of them. I didn't know it at the time, and they would never have spoken of their work, people didn't, but these men, Dilly Knox, Alan Turing, Bill Tutte, the men behind the breaking of Enigma, they were responsible for shortening the war by many years. They were geniuses, intellectual giants. Now, of course, they are all dead and thanks to the Official Secrets Act, many of them have gone to their graves without anyone having the faintest idea of the huge debt we owe them. That is why, Mr Hunter, if occasionally I lose my patience, you will have to forgive a sick and somewhat sentimental old man.' And with that George Wiseman firmly but politely shut the door.

4

Sir John had never behaved like this, never shown such a personal interest in someone before. But then these were exceptional circumstances and he could never have predicted that events would have unfolded quite as they had. He opened his Telegraph and idly scanned the inside pages. Much of the joy of the daily paper had been taken for him years ago. Now there was no need to read a single sensationalist sentence. Anything of any real importance from any publication around the world was first translated, then retyped and left in a folder on his desk each and every morning. He flicked through to the back pages and the sport. Even this gentle pastime had been tarnished for him in recent years with the introduction of the short game. Work was all that was left. Work and his fine collection of tailored suits. Today he had chosen a fitted two button silver-grey number with a dark purple silk lining. A little unusual certainly, but one of his favourites. Yes, now that he was unable to smoke almost anywhere, was forced to watch cricket matches that finished by lunchtime and have all the world's news, threat or no threat, condensed into one pithy sentence, often not even that, most of life's simple pleasures seemed to have been denied him. He'd even lost his inclination to work his way through the typing pool on four. So, work it was. He brushed a dusty blob of London from his lapel and looked over the top of his Telegraph into the next compartment. This lad was doing well. Dangerously well.

Hunter spent the train journey back to Cambridge painstakingly dissecting his encounter with the author George Wiseman. He thought about the flat and the old man's incredible collection of photographs. He remembered their conversations about Enigma, Wiseman's extraordinary revelations regarding the Commonwealth and wondered what had made him suggest he give up on the code. He hoped he'd not upset the old boy, after all it was true, there had been a whole generation to whom Enigma was more than just a puzzle to be solved, more than a sophisticated parlour game. To these people it really had been a matter of life and death.

Knox. Turing. Tutte.

As the scenery flashed by, transporting him from Hertfordshire, through Essex and finally to Cambridgeshire, deep down, in his gut, something stirred. Hunter began to feel profoundly uncomfortable. There was something he had overlooked, like a voice off, lost in the wind Hunter's doubts nipped and worried him. Plagued him. A voice which, in the past he might have tried to shut out with tablets and pills, but which now he was desperate to hear and to comprehend. It called to him, through the sleepless nights and the lingering effects of Wiseman's whisky, always there, yet never present, woolly and indistinct and no matter how much Hunter struggled to organize his thoughts, it would not be heard and so the idea continued to elude him. In an effort to quieten his mind Hunter opened his freshly signed copy of *Setting Europe Ablaze,* idly flicking through its pages without particularly taking anything in. He found with pride the one spelling mistake he had underlined that morning and then turned to the photographs at its centre. It was difficult to imagine the handsome young man sat with his father was the same elderly gentleman with whom he had, somewhat reluctantly, just been drinking whisky.

What had the old fool been talking about? Just before Hunter left Wiseman had suddenly become quite animated and talkative. Perhaps it had been the whisky? Hunter was certain he had little in the way of human contact day to day and that had contributed to his awkwardly aggressive conversational manner. Maybe he had been about to hit his stride when Hunter had decided to leave. He'd given him that great long speech about the code breakers at Bletchley Park and implied, rather bluntly, that Hunter should be a little more respectful. Hunter was prepared to concede that he might have had a point. He knew his history. He knew the debt they were due. Turing had committed suicide, unable to come to terms with his sexuality and had only recently been recognised for his remarkable contributions to the war effort. Similarly, thanks to their unerring devotion to the official secrets act, Hunter knew many others had only been properly recognised either in extreme old age or posthumously. Bill Tutte was one such tragic case. He had gone to his grave having received no official thanks for the ground-breaking work he had undertaken at Station X. Hunter flicked through a few more pages of Wiseman's book. What could they have been talking about, he wondered, for Bill Tutte's name to crop up? Tutte hadn't been involved in the breaking of Enigma, although he had worked at Bletchley Park. Why would the old man have thrown his name in? Surely not a simple mistake? Wiseman knew his history far too well, had been there, possibly even met the man. Maybe the whisky then? Or was the old boy trying deliberately to mislead him, send him down some strange blind alley? Perhaps another test, like the names of the Poles? If so Hunter wanted to go back and put him straight right away. He fought off the last effects of the alcohol. What possible reason could he have had to try and put Bill Tutte's name into his thoughts? And then, like a giant ball of tangled string unravelling, Hunter's mind began to see things more clearly, to hear and understand the voice which had plagued him since leaving South Kensington. He began furiously turning the pages of Wiseman's book back to the glossy collection of black and white photographs at its heart. Bill Tutte had never worked on Enigma. That was the point. That was what Wiseman had been trying to tell him. Bill Tutte had worked on a completely different machine. Lorenz. The machine in the photograph. The coding machine that the twenty-something-year-old George Wiseman had so proudly sat behind with his father. It wasn't an Enigma machine at all. True it wasn't the best photograph that had ever been taken but Hunter couldn't believe he'd missed it. It was a Lorenz machine. Lorenz had been used by the German High Command as an add on to a teleprinter. Lorenz was the machine that Bill Tutte had single-handedly reconstructed without ever having clapped eyes on one. Hunter had not listened carefully enough to the old man, not looked closely enough at the photograph. The machine on the table didn't have Enigma's distinctive keyboard, nor it's wooden carrying box. It was in its appearance an altogether less elegant device, bigger and not designed to be portable for use in the field, being much more at home in an office. Hitler's personal means of communication, his "secret writer", all messages for the eyes of the few, and ten thousand dedicated men and women in a collection of rickety huts in the grounds of an eclectic manor house situated by a moderate sized lake in the Buckinghamshire countryside. Hunter had leapt to a totally false conclusion. But a conclusion based on what? He'd spent the last eighteen months breaking Enigma and so there had been no reason to believe that the code pushed through his letter box had been anything other than just that, another Enigma code, another weather report salvaged from the records of The IWP. The inscription on the photograph in Wiseman's book had said Bletchley Park which had made him think of Enigma and so that was what he had seen, an Enigma machine. The code he'd been sent wasn't an Enigma code, it was from a Lorenz machine and what the boffins at Bletchley had called Fish. He'd been trying to crack the wrong damn code. Traffic sent by the two machines could never have been confused, they were completely different, but that wasn't what Hunter had expected to see and consequently he had seen only what he had wanted to see. Had Wiseman been trying to tell him, trying to steer him in the right direction with his dropping of Bill Tutte's name? Hunter's mind was working at a thousand miles an hour. Now it wasn't about the machine, it was about the technique of encryption. Enigma used a substitution cypher, altering one letter for another, whilst the Lorenz machine had used an additive cypher based on the Vernam code, where one letter was added to another to produce a third. If whoever had written the code had used an additive cypher the results would, to all intense and purposes, look identical to an Enigma code. Hunter prayed he could simply tweak the algorithm to take that into account and the hill climber would take care of the rest.

He found the sheet with its burst of seemingly random characters. If this was a Lorenz code it was quite possibly the first one Hunter had ever seen. Lorenz had only been declassified in 2002 and perhaps due to the overwhelming attention garnered by Enigma, or possibly because of its apparent functionality and ugliness had never made the impression on the public its older, sleeker cousin had. Consequently, not only was this potentially an incredibly rare piece of code, but because Lorenz was the exclusive instrument of the German High Command, Hunter realised, its content could well be extremely important too. It wasn't unheard of for the small team in hut 3 to break messages from the Fuhrer himself.

The biggest single problem Hunter faced was the complete lack of a depth. Wiseman had called it a dead duck, and perhaps he had been right. During the war there had always been some context in which to place the communications; where they were sent to and from, when they were sent, and the ever present possibility that, due to a lazy operator, vital wheel settings had not been changed. Hunter had thought he had nothing, no clues to go on, but then the code must have been transmitted after 1940 when Hitler had contacted the Lorenz Electrical Company in Berlin and commissioned the machine. Additionally, the message probably originated from the Italian Peninsula, the Western Front or Russia and the Eastern Front. It wasn't a lot to go on, and the timeframe was still significantly larger than he would have preferred, but it was more than he had had up until this point. Suddenly Hunter's dreams of Nazi gold, masterpieces secreted in subterranean passages, and missing U-boats, sunk but never found, flooded his mind. And if *he* was excited by the possibilities, Hunter could only imagine how the Professor would feel. Should he phone him immediately to let him know? He would wait. He would wait until he had seen Joth, until he was holding the Fuhrer's personally written message in his hand and then he would go and see Professor Sinclair and present it to him.

Hunter would have to seriously re-gig his program. Amy would be aggravatingly patient and supportive whilst simultaneously quietly seething and furious. Enigma had worked with initially three and then, after the 2nd February 1942 and the German Navy's introduction of the M4, four wheels, producing a daunting 150 million, million starting positions. But Lorenz, an infinitely more complex machine with twelve wheels and 501 pins generated an eyewatering 1.6 quadrillion starting positions. Hunter reassessed his position. Amy would, quite justifiably, not simply be furious. This time, she might just kill him.

Alec Bell was starting to enjoy the trappings of his success. There were the now regular dinner invitations, the international travel, often in first class and more money than he could ever have anticipated, however optimistically. He wasn't wealthy, far from it, but it was a comfortable income for someone of his age, as in addition to his lecturer's salary, revenue was beginning to trickle in from a variety of other sources. The university seemed only too happy to have their latest darling paraded before the press and Alec was certainly not adverse to the publicity, if anything, he thrived on it. They'd arranged a string of interviews with increasingly low brow publications. He'd been encouraged to talk less and less about his ground-breaking mathematical theories and more of his tastes, hobbies and increasingly lavish lifestyle. Ironically this had meant that he had been able to indulge in one of his favourite passions. He'd been one of a very few students to own a car at university, taking huge pleasure in offering lifts to friends in his little Fiat Punto. But now he had the money and the credit rating he'd so long desired, Alec had done the unthinkable. Despite his friends many warnings that he would kill himself at the first busy junction, he'd bought a Starfire blue TVR S3. It was an old car now, never famed for its reliability and initially the insurance payments had been crippling but none of that mattered, not to Alec. He loved the sculptured lines coupled with the raw naked aggression of the V6, and the noise was quite something else. His friends hadn't been the only ones anxious about Alec's safety. Much to Amy's entertainment, at an end of term quad party, a soothsayer who had always claimed to be nothing of the kind, had taken his hand in hers and told Alec he was afraid of death. Alec had tried to laugh it off. Of course he was afraid of death. Wasn't everybody? No, she had said. It is not the moment of death which terrifies you. Not the instant of your demise. That they had been able to agree was nothing more than entropy, a gradual yet inevitable decline and a concept Alec understood only too well. No it was not this which haunted him, it was the running out of time. The thought that there was still more to do. The idea that he might have left great works unfinished. The woman had summed it all up rather cruelly Alec thought.

I think you're scared the world will forget you once you're gone.

And so, upon reflection, Alec had sworn that, although he thought the sentiment mawkish and clawing, he would live each hour as if it were his last, he would cram every day with excitement and adventure. The S3 growled beneath him like a hunted animal.

He was parking up having taken Jolanta out for a spin in the Cambridge countryside in the morning followed by lunch in a sleepy little village near Huntingdon. The purpose had been twofold. Whilst he'd been trying to impress the twenty-year-old undergraduate and get her into bed, Alec had also wanted to give the TVR a good run out on Cambridgeshire's tightly bending country lanes. He was confident Jolanta was coming round but now he had papers that needed working on for a particularly important series of lectures. An agent would be present and there had been talk of television. Alec was fast becoming one of the new breed of media driven intellectuals, always willing to be interviewed and ready with a quotable soundbite. The S3 suited him nicely. It always attracted onlookers and so he wasn't surprised to feel that someone was staring at him now. He took his case from the passenger seat next to him and swung his legs out. His only surprise, to find it was Professor Frederick Sinclair admiring his car.

'So, this is how you get around, Alec?'

'Beautiful isn't she?'

Sinclair eyed the car.

'I'm not convinced she is a thing of beauty, nor for that matter that she is a she. I would say this however, *it*, whatever it may be, is extremely noisy. Are you walking?'

They set off towards the college debating the most recent scandal to befall its Dean.

'I expect your name will be at the top of many people's lists,' Alec said.

'Well, that is most flattering to hear, but we both know that these appointments are never straight forward. It may well drag on for some time. In my experience they rarely, if ever, go to the most deserving or well qualified candidate.'

Once inside the two men turned to go their separate ways.

'By the bye, have you seen Scott recently?' Sinclair asked.

'Just the other day as a matter of fact.'

'And how is he?'

'You know I'm looking for an assistant? I thought he'd come to ask for a job.'

'But he hadn't?'

'No. Too tied up busting codes for you.'

'Well Alec, that is his choice.'

'Sure. I'm just a bit concerned it seems to be taking up all of his time.'

'Really?'

'He needs to get out there, look for some work.'

'Naturally. I shouldn't imagine he'll have to wait very long before he's approached by someone. You didn't.'

'Question is, will Amy be prepared to wait?'

'Ah yes,' Sinclair said, 'I do see.'

'He's off to London to talk to some crusty old fart about codes.'

'Crusty old fart?' Sinclair asked, annunciating each word scrupulously.

'No offence. I think he told Amy he's got a job interview, but actually he's off seeing this author guy.'

'I see.'

'Amy's going to be so pissed off when she finds out.'

'Indeed. Well, it has been charming catching up with you Mr Bell, we shall keep an eye on Scott.'

✳✳✳

Hunter raced back to the house. Joth was sitting at the kitchen table nursing a cold cup of tea and trawling the property section of the local paper.

'Got another one for you,' Hunter said peering over his shoulder.

'Fine,' the South African replied circling a flat on the Madingley Road, 'just not in the middle of the night, please.'

'Seen Amy?'

'Upstairs. I think she's had your father on the phone again?'

'You going somewhere?'

Joth closed the paper. He was starting to resent being stuck in the middle of Scott and Amy's tempestuous relationship. There was a one bed-flat which he'd discounted as too small, but now was looking more and more appealing. The idea of shutting out the world and in particular Scott Hunter, was looking extremely attractive indeed. He would do this one last translation for him. It would draw a neat line under their time as flatmates together and then he would move on and out.

'Where is it then?'

'What?'

'The text!'

'I don't have it, yet. Couple of days tops.'

With a little luck Joth might have a flat lined up by then.

***

As soon as he saw Amy, Hunter knew she was upset.

'So, how did you get on?' she asked pointedly.

'Good. Very good actually,' he said setting up the MacBook on his desk.

'Did you get the job then? In London?'

Hunter put the machine on to charge and in an effort to appear casual began searching through his bookcase.

'Too early to say,' he offered over his shoulder.

'What about Alec?'

'I spoke to him. I said I would.'

Amy stood in front of him now, blocking his way to the desk and his laptop. 'I know Scott, because I spoke to him as well. He told me he offered you a job and you turned him down. You turned him down! What the hell were you thinking?'

'You called him?'

'To see if you got the job, yes.'

Hunter couldn't believe what he was hearing.

'He told me about London too, Scott. There was no interview, was there? You lied to me.'

She'd gone behind his back and spoken to Alec, and then Alec had, feeling unable to keep his mouth shut, dropped him in it and from a considerable height. Hunter didn't want to think about any motivation Alec might have had for such an act.

'I love you Scott, but I can't cope with this. How am I supposed to know if I can trust you? I've had your dad on the phone asking how you are and when you're ever going to call him back and I'm getting pretty sick of trying to reassure him you're okay. I think *he's* even more worried about you than I am.'

'I know. I'm sorry.' Another lie. 'Why don't we go out tomorrow night, have a meal. It'll give us a chance to sit and talk.'

'All right,' Amy said unsurely, then picked up her handbag and left.

✳✳✳

In spite of their row it wasn't long before Hunter was poring over Philip Rutherland's *Enigma.* He quickly found the Lorenz schematics in the appendices at the back. The scale of the machine's workings was bewildering. He'd been impressed with Enigma, but never daunted by it, and now he was wondering if Lorenz might not just be beyond him. He sat as the evening sun streamed in through his window and thought about Amy and then Lorenz and then Amy again. He'd gone too far this time, he knew that, but if he could just get the new settings right and onto the computer before she returned then maybe he would call it a day. He'd take her to the best restaurant he could afford, wine and dine her and win her back. Perhaps he'd even phone his father, if that was what it would take.

By the time he'd finished writing the new code it was late and he was tired. Hunter was about to set the programme running when Alec came to mind. His so called friend who it appeared had gone behind his back and told Amy what he was up to. He half considered not sharing the algorithm, but then there had been more then enough lies and broken promises for one day. He went into the MacBook's applications folder and found the file, dragged it over to the dropbox icon where it disappeared. Then he created a new file called *Blonde Twins* and copied in the algorithm and all its supporting files. Alec also used a Mac so he would have no problems in opening and running them. All that remained was the simple task of inviting him to share the file's contents. Dropbox created an email for him, he clicked "Approve" and off it went.

Time to see if his suspicions were correct. He input the 51 characters and hit the return key. The familiar pattern of figures appeared and immediately started tumbling down the screen. Hunter felt sure this would break it, so why was there still that nagging doubt? Less so than before admittedly, but still that bothersome voice whispering that he'd missed something. All was not quite right. However, he wasn't going to work it out now and in any case he could hear Amy creaking up the stairs. He quickly undressed and jumped in to bed.

The following morning Hunter lay in bed and watched Amy dress for work. She'd come back from the shower, a towel wrapped around her chest, another piled high on the top of her head in some mysterious knot that only women understood. She let the other towel slip to the floor. Hunter couldn't help but admire her slender figure as she put on her underwear. Then a simple white long sleeved top under her charcoal grey suit. She bent forward before the full-length mirror, shaking the towel from her head, letting her long hair fall loose before drying it and nimbly twisting and tying it behind her head. Hunter was pleased to see she wore the necklace he had given her. Then, rather pointedly he thought, she picked up the towels and dropped them into the laundry basket.

'Are we going out tonight?' he asked as cheerily as he could.

'I don't know, are we?'

'Yes. We need to talk.'

'I agree.' Amy said, clearly still not in the mood to make life easy for him.

'Leave it with me, I'll book us a table somewhere nice. Italian?'

'Fine,' she replied frostily. 'See you later then.' She was at the window, smoothing out some paperwork he should probably have dealt with. 'Your laptop's doing something odd,' she added.

Hunter leapt out of bed, kissed her goodbye, pulled on an old Joy Division t-shirt that he found lying on the floor and sat by his MacBook. It appeared that the algorithm had done its work. He moved the icon over the decode tab. One click and the screen changed instantly to reveal the plain text.

There would be no need for Joth's linguistic skills today. You didn't need to be a language student to recognise a list of names when you saw one, even if some of them did appear to be Russian or Polish. There were six in total;

J K Borkowski

P Utkin

D J Metzger

H Schmid

J A Seidel
F Ritthaler

Hunter stared long and hard at the screen. He didn't know how to feel. Confused? Certainly. A little disappointed? Possibly. A name with no reference points was just that and nothing more. A name. It was no wonder the programme had struggled to decode it, the algorithm was far better suited to words and phrases. Proper nouns were infinitely harder to accommodate because they had little inherent pattern. These people could have been anyone. Heroes, traitors, politicians or footballers. Hunter couldn't even tell if they were male or female, dead or alive. Perhaps it would help if he printed the list out and looked at it in a hard state. No, it was still just a list of names. Were any of them similar in anyway? Not particularly. He ran them through the google search engine. Apart from Julie Ann Seidel who, according to her Facebook page, was a seventeen-year-old girl living in Sacramento and whose relationship status was '"uncertain", there was no sign of any of them on the internet. Hunter assumed the Californian teenager just happened to share the same surname and initials. Now that was odd wasn't it? These days it was almost impossible not to leave some footprint of your life on the world wide web whether it be intentionally or not. That suggested these people might have predated the internet, although with all the various web sites devoted to tracking down long-lost relatives and plotting family trees, that too seemed improbable. After much thought, Hunter conceded the only thing he understood with any degree of certainty, was just how little he understood.

He packed up his things, put the laptop in his bag along with the code and the hard copy of the list. Professor Sinclair would know what to make of it, that had always been the way their relationship had worked. Hunter would do the number crunching and Sinclair would make sense of the results. Quite suddenly he needed to get out of the house. On and off he'd been staring at a computer screen for hours. A break from it all would do him good. He'd buy a paper and sit by his favourite cherry tree in Fellows' Gardens, then grab the professor sometime around lunch when he ought to be free.

On his way out he ran into Joth pouring over his laptop at the kitchen table. Seeing Hunter, the South African quickly shut the computer down.

'What happened with the code?'

'Good question. Just a load of names. Listen, sorry it's been a bit mad around here with me and Amy. We're sorting it out, okay?'

'Cheers man.' Joth brushed his sandy blond hair back, 'Might catch you later?'

Hunter stopped at the arcade of shops at the end of their street. He tried to support it in all its faded splendour. There was a faceless supermarket around the corner which was really hammering small businesses and now the local community didn't even have a proper post office. He ducked in to get his copy of The Times and some stamps, then a short walk to the bus stop and into Cambridge. Once he'd got his ticket he'd give Wiseman a call and thank him for the tip off.

The top of the bus was quieter at this time of day. The school run had finished and so Hunter had it almost entirely to himself. He briefly toyed with starting the crossword before instead electing to quickly skim the day's news. Hunter took out his iPhone and scrolled through the contact list. Wiseman.

'Hullo, who is this?'

'Mr Wiseman, it's Scott Hunter here.'

'Yes, Mr Hunter and how may I help you today?' Hunter was getting used to Wiseman's misanthropic telephone manner.

'I just wanted to thank you for seeing me yesterday and for your help.'

'I wasn't aware I'd been any.'

'Oh, yes. I had a long think about what you said and… well, I've had a bit of a break through actually.'

'I see.'

'Thanks to you I realised it wasn't an Enigma code at all.'

'Really?'

'It must have been sent on a Lorenz machine.'

'Good Heavens, are you quite sure?'

'Positive. I've already broken it.'

'How unusual. And was it anything of interest?'

'I'm not sure I'd call it interesting exactly. Unusual maybe?'

'How so?'

'It's just a list. A list of foreign names.'

Hunter heard something change and then silence.

'Mr Wiseman, are you there?'

'Names, you say?'

'German mostly but one or two which could be Polish or Russian I suppose. Hang on I've got it here,' Hunter found the print out in his bag, 'Borkowski, Utkin, Metzger, Schmid... Mr Wiseman? Mr Wiseman?' The phone was dead. Hunter checked. There was a full signal but Mr George Wiseman was no longer on the other end of the line. Perhaps he'd been moving between areas when they had been cut off? But even as Hunter was thinking it, he knew that George Wiseman had just put the phone down on him. He flicked back to recent calls and rang the number again. Wiseman answered immediately.

'Where are you?' There was a degree of urgency to his voice which Hunter had never heard before.

'On a bus going into town, Mr Wise...'

'Where's the code?' The old man cut him short before he'd had time to finish.

'Right here, I was ...'

'Don't go into town. Get off the bus. Do not go home.'

'What?'

'Listen to me, it is imperative you do not go home, do you understand me? You will have to find somewhere else. Somewhere safe. And do not ring me again,' and then the phone went dead for a second time. Hunter stared at it in disbelief.

Last number dialled. Redial. He brushed the icon with his thumb. A slight wait whilst the connection was made and then the engaged tone. He tried again and again and got the same result. What the hell was going on? Wiseman had either immediately phoned someone else or deliberately left his phone off the hook. Either way it seemed the old goat was losing his marbles. But on the other hand, he had seemed genuinely concerned. *Imperative* he'd said. Now Hunter began to worry. He could see a bus stop fast approaching. Perhaps he should do something just in case the old man hadn't gone completely off his rocker. He pressed the yellow stop button. An ugly electronic bell rang out and the bus began to slow.

Hunter weighed up his options. He tried Wiseman's phone for a fourth time but the result was no different. He knew this bus route pretty well. He'd gone three stops, but if he crossed the road he might have to wait a good half hour for the next service. It would be quicker if he just started back home on foot.

Do not go home, do you understand me?

Wiseman might be concerned but he knew nothing about Hunter or his home. In fact, the more Hunter considered it, the surer he was that Wiseman had no idea where he lived. Surely these were the overreactions of an aged and possibly slightly confused old man. Hunter thought of his papa and how there were times even when he was lucid he could confuse the simplest things. Not to mention, it was entirely possible that Wiseman had already started drinking.

Once he'd negotiated the roundabout and started along Danforth Road he was able to see the front of his house. And once he could see the front of his house Hunter knew something was wrong. First there were the bins. They had been moved and were partially blocking the short flagstone path. Then, he realised the front door was slightly ajar. It didn't appear to have been forced but he couldn't think of any reason for it to have been left open. He was sure he had felt it close firmly behind him. Hunter's heart was racing. Nervously he stood in the house's dilapidated old porch, gently pushing at the door. Something was preventing it from opening. Using both hands Hunter pushed a little harder. The door gave, but still not enough to allow him entry. He took a step back, held himself for a moment and then, with one quick step, thrust his shoulder firmly against the old front door. There was a sickening sound as it shuddered briefly before revealing Joth's prone body, bent and lifeless and lying at a peculiarly Dutch angle, his knee unnaturally twisted and broken, a neatly cauterized hole in the centre of his forehead where the brass 9 millimetre bullet had entered.

Hunter's head buzzed and thrummed. Colour left him, his perceptions diminishing to featureless shades of grey. Noises from the road vanished, his spine prickling hot whilst his body simultaneously cold and numb. Hunter realised there was every chance he was about to faint. He grabbed at the staircase's newel post, steadying himself, forcing oxygen into his lungs. His head was swimming with images; the night Joth had helped Amy home after a college party, the intense sporting rivalry, always played out at their local pub and in front of a gigantic screen, his heartfelt sadness when Mandela had passed.

And then, nothing. A sudden and quite inexorable nothingness. No sight, no sound, no hot, no cold, no feeling. Nothing at all. And just as quickly, as though from a great distance, noises came rushing back at him. Colours flooded his world. He still felt a little unsteady but he was pretty sure he would not now faint. He looked at Joth's lifeless body. Jesus Christ.

Hunter's mind was still racing. Was it possible that whoever had done this was still in the house? Surely they had heard him come in? He reached into his back pocket, withdrew his iPhone and switched it to silent. What on earth would he do if he encountered someone wielding a gun, carry on into the house or turn tail and run, run as fast as he was able?

Hunter stepped over his friend's prone body and into the house's cramped hallway. From here he could see a little way into the kitchen. That appeared to be much as he had left it, so he began to slowly climb the stairs. He checked over his shoulder, making sure he'd not imagined the scene in the hallway. From this angle he could clearly see a pool of fresh blood forming behind Joth's head, tainting his beautiful blonde hair. Stepping over a loose board Hunter reached the kink in the stairs and was able to see the landing for the first time. Both bedroom doors had been left flung open, but no sounds came from within. He edged up the final few stairs, all the while ready to turn tail and run for his life.

Joth's bedroom was at the back of the house, overlooking their sadly neglected postage stamp of a garden. Hunter squinted between the door and its jam. It appeared empty, so he tentatively edged inside. T-shirts, underwear, text books all littered the floor. Joth's papers covered every available surface as if incautiously thrown from some central point and allowed to settle like furiously conceived confetti. However, Hunter was regrettably forced to concede, none of this was necessarily the work of an armed intruder. His now dead friend's room was often in such a state of disarray it was impossible to say whether it had been disturbed or not. Then he saw it, lying next to his unmade bed, Joth's beloved copy of Faust, its cover crumpled and torn. Someone had definitely been here. Joth would never have discarded this particular book so carelessly. Next Hunter moved to the bathroom which he could see was empty. That just left his bedroom at the front of the house.

He edged along the back of their bedroom door. If he could get a little closer he'd be able to use Amy's six foot cheval mirror to see the opposite side of the room. Light was streaming in through the window at the front of the house and Hunter could just make out his desk. Again, papers everywhere, books lying open and hastily discarded. Some had fallen, landing unnaturally, their pages bending and folding. He could see the far side of the room now. His bookcase had been all but completely emptied onto the floor, his bedside cabinet turned upside down. Crucially the room was empty, and for the first time Hunter felt he could breathe a little easier. Clearly whoever had been there had been looking for something *he* possessed and following his conversation with George Wiseman it was obvious it had to be the list. But why? Why would anyone be interested in a list of foreign names?

Hunter was just about to consider his next move when he heard the living room door below him open and then shut again. Then footsteps from downstairs. The living room! How had he been so stupid? They'd been in there all this time. His heart started to race again and then he heard the front door carefully being pulled to. Hunter was already at the window. Cautiously he leant forward just in time to catch sight of the back of a man's shaven head. Hunter was grateful he'd not encountered him with or without a gun. He looked enormous. In one hand a dull black firearm. Hunter knew very little about guns, but he'd watched enough films to recognise a pistol with a silencer when he saw one. A powerful arm shot out and easily shoved the brown recycling bin out of his way. A flash of silver. A silver wedding ring, above it a tattoo Hunter couldn't quite make out but which seemed to stop abruptly at the wrist like a shirt, and travelled up the man's left arm before disappearing under a black t-shirt. He watched as the man shot a look up the road and then disappeared behind a row of trees. There was the sound of a door slamming and a car driving off.

Hunter pulled up a chair and sat down. His legs felt weak, his heart was pounding. He needed to take stock. On the table lay all his notes, his ring binder roughly opened and then discarded, computer discs scattered here and there. And then he saw it. The last thing the killer had seen in their bedroom. A letter to Amy from her work offering her longer hours and a meeting to discuss any National Insurance or income tax ramifications. At the top, in large clear print the address of her offices.

'Amy?'

'Scott, what is it, I'm kind of busy?'

'Listen, you're going to have to trust me and do as I say.'

'I beg your pardon?'

'Meet me at the railway station now.'

'Scott, what are you talking about? I'm at work, you know that.'

He started to raise his voice.

'Amy, go to the station as quickly as you can. I'll explain everything when I see you. I've never asked you to do anything like this before. Please trust me and get there as soon as you can, okay?'

'All right Scott, but you're kind of freaking me out.'

'Just do it.'

Hunter needed to move quickly. He saw Wiseman's book carelessly thrown on the floor, and shoved it in his shoulder bag. In the kitchen, next to his house keys he found Joth's wallet. Hunter didn't hesitate. He put that in his bag too. Any thoughts that it could have been a burglary gone wrong now put completely from his mind. Then Hunter phoned the emergency services and reported a fire at the premises.

The house next door was rented by a group of students. Hunter took a quick look over their front wall confident at what he would find. A bicycle.

Amy was already waiting under one of the arches outside Cambridge Station when he arrived. He abandoned the bike with the hundreds of others and rushed to her.

'Are you all right?' He took her in his arms holding her tight.

'Scott, what the hell is going on? I'm going to have to get back to work and...'

'Joth's dead.'

As he'd cycled from the house to the station he had gone through all the ways he would break the news to her. What he hadn't wanted to do was blurt it out.

'What? What did you say?' Amy half smiled at him. This was some terrible idea of a joke, a sick prank. But as she looked at his face there was no sign of him relenting.

'It's Joth. Oh God Amy I'm so sorry. Joth's dead. He's been shot.'

'Are you sure?'

'I found him.'

'Oh my God. Well, shouldn't you be with the police?'

'You don't understand Amy. I think it should have been me.'

'What?'

'There isn't time to explain. We need to get as far away from here as we can and quickly.'

'But Scott,' she was looking at him pleadingly now, on the verge of tears.

'Amy, you've got to trust me, we're both in danger and we need to leave now.' He took her arm and guided her towards the station.

'Where are we going? I need to call the office.'

'There's no time. The first train leaves for Kings Cross in three minutes. That'll have to do. I'll explain everything I can once we're on it, now go.'

Hunter spent the journey into London comforting Amy and gently relating to her exactly what he had discovered on returning to their house. He told her everything, how he'd found the code on their doormat, his lunch with Alec, the subsequent trip to London and his meeting with the author George Wiseman. He'd struggled to describe the irascible old man, explaining how he felt he might have helped, whether consciously or not, to break the code. And finally he read her the list of names his algorithm had produced, all the while praying silently that she would have an answer, a solution to it all. Then, when she tearfully admitted to being as bewildered as he was, he persuaded her to drink some sweet tea from the trolley and close her eyes. An hour and a half later they stood beneath the flickering information board at Kings Cross Station.

'We have to go to South Ken.,' Amy said.

'Wiseman?'

'He clearly knows something, you said so yourself.'

'You haven't met him. He's a throw back. A relic of the Cold War. He lives in this ridiculous apartment in one of the flashiest parts of London. I'm sorry but you don't afford that writing whimsical reminiscences about your father and the Second World War.'

'Let me meet him?'

'He won't tell you anything. He's all paranoid and unhelpful.'

'That's why we need to go and see him. We need to find out exactly what it is he knows.'

'But Amy, even if I felt that we could trust him, which I don't, he won't tell us anything. He could be involved for all we know.'

She looked up at Hunter, her eyes still red from crying but soft and kind. 'Let me meet him. I'm a fairly good judge of character, wouldn't you say?' She bent forward to kiss him. 'Poor Joth,' she said quietly.

5

For the second time in as many days Scott Hunter watched as the heavy curtain lifted and just as quickly fell back into place again. The briefest glimpse of the man inside. A hand, a cuff, a flash of jewellery the only signs of occupancy. Wiseman observed them dispassionately from his fortress and then Hunter listened impatiently as Amy attempted to persuade the grand old man to permit them entry.

'We desperately need your help?'

'I can't help you, I told Mr Hunter that. You have no right coming here. No right at all. I'm a sick old man, so please leave me alone, or I shall be forced to telephone the police.' But Wiseman was sounding anything but sick or old.

'We just want to talk to you.'

'There's nothing more to be said. That young man should never have...'

'Please will you let us in? Something's happened.'

Silence as Wiseman contemplated Amy's last roll of the dice.

'Very well young lady.' The entry buzzer sounded and Hunter pushed past her and inside.

The door to Wiseman's flat opened just enough that he could address them over the taught silver security chain.

'What do you want?'

'Answers.'

'Answers to what?'

'You know damn well.'

George thrust out a confident pad and guided the delivery away. He was not going to be dictated to by this young pup and his companion. 'You said something had happened?'

'Yes.'

'You went home?'

'Yes, I fucking well went home, and do you know what I found? My best friend with his brains blown out, so *you* had better start coming up with some answers otherwise I will be the one going to the police.'

'Shot?'

'Yes, by a giant with a shaven head.'

Hunter observed Wiseman's face. An involuntary flicker of what, emotion, remorse? he couldn't say, but in that moment of morbid revelation, he was certain Wiseman changed.

'You had better come in.'

Hunter gave Amy an exasperated look as the old man pushed the door to and then removed the security chain.

'You saw his killer?'

'Leaving, yes. After he'd turned our bedroom upside down. Looking for this I presume.' Hunter handed Wiseman the list of names and as he took the page in his bent and brittle fingers it was as if the elderly gentleman shrunk before their eyes. His shoulders drooped and Amy noticed his hand begin to tremble. They followed him into the front room where he immediately went to pour himself a drink.

'Let me do that,' she said taking the decanter from Wiseman's shaking hand, 'you sit down.' Amy's eyes travelled to Hunter's and she silently begged him to take it easy. Then without asking she splashed some whisky into three glasses whilst George lead Hunter away.

'How did you get here?'

'Train.'

'Which train?'

'The quarter past from Cambridge.'

'Where did it get in?'

'Liverpool Street.'

'Then what did you do?'

'The tube.'

'Christ. Which tube? Circle line or through town?'

'We took the Central line to Holborn and then changed to the Piccadilly, I think.'

Wiseman snatched at the glass Amy offered.

'You think?'

'Yes, the Piccadilly Line.'

'Were you followed?'

'Were we what?'

'Followed. Followed.'

'How the hell should we know?' Amy chipped in a little resentfully.

'Did you see any one consistently on your journey across London? Someone you might have seen on the train from Cambridge? Were you followed?'

'Scott, what is this all about?'

Wiseman was in Hunter's face, ignoring Amy's brief protestation, any fleeting moment of weakness long forgotten. 'Were you followed?'

'I don't know,' Hunter offered meekly.

'Christ. All right. What about the tube. Which station did you come from?'

'Gloucester Road.'

'Then straight up Queen's Gate?'

'Of course,' Amy put in, missing the point.

'Is this relevant?' Hunter asked.

'To me, extremely, yes.'

'Look, I don't know if we were followed or not. I'd like to know why my friend was killed for this though,' Hunter said gesturing to the page Wiseman still clutched, 'and I'm guessing you had something to do with it.'

'I don't know what you're talking about. I've never seen this before.'

'I'm afraid I don't believe you George. Not only do I not believe you but I think you know exactly who these people are, or were.'

Amy gave the two men another healthy scotch and quietly insisted that Hunter try to calm down, but to little avail.

'All right. Let me tell you what I know,' he continued. 'I received an unbreakable code a couple of days ago. It came to me from god knows who with not a scratch of information on it except my name on the envelope. Then I came out here to see you and you were pretty damn cagey. But just before you ushered me out you let something slip, didn't you? You brought up Bill Tutte. Now why did you do that, I wonder? He never worked on Enigma, as I'm sure you knew, but he did work on Lorenz. I could have put that down to a simple slip, but then I recalled that little speech you gave. A young man in the company of his wartime heroes, you said. A little more respect for their sacrifice, you said. Surely you remember? What could have made you think of Bill Tutte and Lorenz if you'd genuinely never seen this before?' Hunter said holding up the original.

'Young man, I have seen hundreds, possibly even thousands of such codes. I think you will agree with me, that in one respect they are all identical. You talked to me of their beauty. In a sense that is their beauty is it not? Nothing can be gleaned from them, they are simply as they are, a string of letters.' Wiseman fixed Hunter with an unequivocal stare and jabbed a crooked finger at him. 'The code you showed me yesterday looked no different to any of the other hundreds I have seen. I was as fooled by it as you clearly were.'

'Why did you suggest the Lorenz machine then?'

'I didn't, not intentionally. I simply thought it was an avenue you might wish to explore. Nothing more, nothing less.'

'But you admit you tried to guide me towards Lorenz?'

Wiseman screwed up his face and fiddled with his hearing aid. 'Guide, suggest, advise? I don't recall.'

'And I don't buy it,' Hunter said shaking his head.

'I'm afraid that is the truth, whether you *buy* it or not. You will see, if you choose to think about it that no two codes are the same, yet they are all identical in their appearance. Am I not correct?'

Hunter understood the old man perfectly. When you looked at a page, unless you had a photographic memory, they did all seem the same. You might remember the first four or five letters but after that it would take an incredible act of concentration to remember even ten letters. Perhaps there was some truth in what the old man said. But there was still that niggling doubt.

'When I called you, you told me not to go home. Why? You must have recognised the names? These people, who are they?'

'I've never heard of them.'

'So why the warning?'

'Just a feeling.'

'Rubbish. You don't do feelings any more than I do.' Hunter blanched on hearing his murdered friend's aphorism. 'Sorry George, you may not have recognised the code, but you sure as hell recognise those names, don't you? Something about that list really got you rattled. You put the phone down on me. Do you remember that?'

Whilst the two men had been talking Amy had been looking over the photographs on the piano. She'd found some of George Wiseman in uniform, doing his National Service. Then, she discovered, there was another side to the man. A picture of him coming out of a church with his bride on his arm, flowers in her hand and confetti in the air. She'd found pictures of him at a typewriter too, next to him an ashtray overflowing with cigarette butts. A book launch, George behind a huge table, books stacked high and a young lady craning forward, Amy imagined, asking for a dedication. There was George lying on the deck of a yacht, propped up on one elbow, the other hand holding a cigarette, a smile of intense happiness on his face and the sea wind blowing in his hair. Bloody Hell, she thought as she carefully picked up one silver framed portrait.

'Is this you with Jean Seberg?'

George replaced the cigar he had been about to light and joined Amy at the piano, relieved to be away from Hunter.

'Indeed it is,' he said taking the photograph from her. 'She was working on a film I was advising on. Nothing came of it in the end, the film I mean. She was kind enough to have her picture taken with me. A charming lady. Such a tragedy, the manner of her passing.'

Wiseman was talking about Jean Seberg as though they were old friends.

'I must say I'm surprised at someone of your age knowing who she is,' he continued.

'Of course I know who she is. She was in Breathless and Joan of Arc.'

'A tragically short career.'

Amy started looking through the rest of the pictures. There were more, Claudia Cardinale, Tina Louise and Anita Ekberg. George, in his day, had clearly been quite the ladies' man.

'What exactly was it you said you did Mr Wiseman?'

'I was lucky enough to have been quintessentially English at a time when it was a blessing and not the curse it has become in more recent years.'

'And you met all of these people?' She cast her hand around the array of Hollywood starlets adorning Wiseman's piano.

'As I said, I was extremely fortunate.' The elderly man smiled, bowing modestly.

Amy had a million questions. She hardly knew where to begin. She'd never met anyone who had actually worked in Hollywood before, let alone a Hollywood unadulterated by green screen and CGI. The Hollywood she adored, when film stars had really been stars and worthy of the epithet. She continued to look through the pictures of her heroes. And then she spotted it. The photograph Hunter had shown her on the train. The photograph Hunter had told her was at the heart of it all. Except it wasn't. Not quite. The one in the book had shown George and his father sat proudly behind the ugly machine with the strange name, but this was a larger picture. The one in the book had been cropped. This one contained more people. A group of six stood in a row behind the Wisemans. Five men and a woman. Amy picked it up.

'I've seen this before haven't I? Isn't it in your book?'

'Is it?' asked Wiseman taking it from her a little too firmly, whilst in the same breath acknowledging his deceit. 'Mr Hunter,' he called over his shoulder, compounding the lie, 'I feel we could all do with something to eat. If you would be so kind as to go into my kitchen where you will find some bread and cheese. Would you mind making us up some sandwiches? This charming young lady has had a terrible shock and is no doubt in need of sustenance.'

Hunter wasn't overly keen on being ordered around like a skivvy, but he had to admit he'd not eaten all day and suspected that neither had Amy. Wiseman waited until he had left the room before returning the picture to the piano.

'You know he thinks you're a spy, don't you?'

Wiseman coughed quietly and Amy wondered if he had heard her at all. He gripped the lid of the piano, his head slowly nodding, moist lips moving silently, as he contemplated his return. Play with a straight bat, take no chances, always think of the long game, come out fighting, try and drive it back over the bowler's head and to hell with the consequences or George's particular favourite, the subtle nick past third man, the cunning feint, the infuriating deflection, the elegant deceit.

'Mr Hunter has what we used to call, an over active imagination,' he said, dabbing at the crease, 'I am an author and occasional script doctor, who in an earlier life did his bit for King and Country, as I should say, did everyone at that time. As a writer I developed something of a reputation, I suppose, but these days I'm seldom read and never quoted.' Watching the ball gently trickle over the boundary rope for four he took Amy's arm and lead her towards the empty fireplace and away from the piano. 'Now, you see' he continued, gesturing at the mantle piece, 'I have other distractions.'

'Your grandchildren?'

Wiseman smiled weakly before coughing noisily into his handkerchief.

'I don't see them as often as I'd like it's true. They all seem to live such a long way away and their parents, well let's just say they aren't so keen on London.'

He took her glass and freshened both their drinks. Amy could see the next question coming a long time before George actually asked it.

'Have you any plans, to start a family I mean?'

'We've only just left college, George.'

'Forgive me that was extremely rude and certainly none of my business.'

Amy waved him off. She was flattered he'd felt able to ask and was starting to understand why George appeared in the company of quite so many beautiful women.

'I think I'd like to have a career first, but yes, maybe, one day.'

'I understand. Tell me a little about Scott.'

No one had ever asked her so directly before. It threw her a little.

'He's funny and frustrating and brilliant and lazy.' George smiled, 'God, did I just say all that? He is lazy though at some things, but others he takes so seriously, like this bloody Enigma thing,' she finished crossly. 'And now Joth's dead and I just don't know what to think. Scott's certain whoever did it was after him.'

'Is he? And has he spoken to his parents, since...'

She shook her head, 'He doesn't speak to his father.'

'Might I ask why that is?'

'And he won't talk to me about it either.'

'That is a shame. I'm afraid my dear that a son's relationship with his father can be every bit as complex as a daughter's, more so, in my experience. At the end of the day all any father really wants is for his son to have a happier life than he has. We may not always achieve this but it is what we all want. I'm certain Scott's father is no different than any other in that respect.'

Before Amy was able to press him any further Hunter returned with a handful of plates and found a space for them by the window.

'I've used up the end of a cucumber I found in your fridge, I hope you don't mind?'

He drew back the curtains, looking up Lansdowne Terrace, drinking in the last of the day's sun.

'Would you mind not doing that?' Wiseman was at his side now, taking the curtain from him and pulling it back into place. 'I don't wish to appear over sensitive, but I do value my privacy. Thank you for taking care of things in the kitchen. Now, once you've finished your sandwiches of course, I expect you'll be wanting to get on your way. The evening is upon us and I should imagine the trains don't run forever, do they?'

Amy looked at him incredulously. The amiable old gentleman who had been chatting so easily with her about her plans for the future had vanished. This man was hard, unforgiving and unwelcoming, no longer the charming womanizer who had enquired so kindly of her ambitions to start a family.

'But George,' she began, 'I thought you understood. We have nowhere to go?'

'What about your parents?'

'They're in Casciano. Tuscany.'

'In which case their house here will be vacant, will it not?' Wiseman pressed.

'Let out for the summer.'

'Mr Hunter, do you not have any family you could call upon?'

'Out of the question.'

'Then where were you planning on staying, if I may ask?'

'Right here. I think it's the least you can do, don't you?' Hunter replied without thinking.

Wiseman shuffled awkwardly for a moment and Hunter wondered if the old boy had heard him properly.

'I'm not entirely sure I appreciate your tone and in any case I'm afraid I do not have a guest bedroom to offer you.'

'We can sleep on the sofa, or Amy can at least.'

'That is completely out of the question. You will have to get a room in a hotel for the night. You will see there are plenty down towards Gloucester Road.'

Hunter looked at Wiseman and forced himself to remember that this was a frail old man.

'Do you have any idea of the price of a room round here, even for only one night? This is bloody Kensington in case you'd forgotten.' Hunter threw back the remainder of his scotch and reached for the decanter. 'All we're asking for is a corner of blanket and at a stretch a pillow. Once we've had a chance to think I promise we'll be out of your way first thing in the morning. I don't want to spend any more time here than is absolutely necessary, believe me.'

They sat in silence and ate Hunter's sandwiches and then Wiseman disappeared only to return with an armful of bedding.

'For you my dear,' he said, handing it to Amy. She made herself comfortable on the sofa whilst the two men sat quietly and drank. As she slowly drifted off to sleep Wiseman turned to his young pup.

'It's a solitary profession you know?'

Hunter thought he did know, but he wasn't quite ready to play along.

'Writing?'

'No, Scott. Not writing.'

Hunter nodded grimly, his suspicions at least partially confirmed. The two men watched over Amy as she slipped further into sleep. The whisky was nearly at an end. George took up the decanter and left, Hunter presumed to refill it. He slipped off his shoes, arranged his and Amy's coats next to the sofa and curled up like a guard dog. He was not quite asleep when George Wiseman returned. The elderly gentleman went to the window and briefly drew back the curtain. The decanter replenished and satisfied by what he had seen, Wiseman poured himself one last scotch before picking up the telephone.

'I have them both,' were the last words Hunter heard as he fell asleep.

6

God he was anxious. He thought he'd feel a little apprehensive today and that that would be quite natural, but he hadn't expected to feel anything like this. Chris Wilson was a bag of nerves. He hadn't slept all night, tossing and turning until his wife had pleaded with him to go and sleep in the other room. The lack of a good night's rest was nothing new, two kids had seen to that. The last time either he or Trish had had a proper night's sleep was when her parents had come up to London for the weekend so they could spend a night away in a hotel in Brighton. Now Ben and Sophie were fussing around him as he tried to make breakfast.

'Daddy, are you really going to be on the tele?'

Christ, that had never even crossed his mind.

'I don't know poppet. Will you be good for mummy while you wait for me?' But Sophie's attention had already moved on to something new.

He doled out a serving of porridge and cut up a banana to go on top, then a spoonful of honey. Trish was in their tiny South London galley kitchen shooing the kids away.

'How are you feeling?'

'Sick.'

Before they'd decided to have a family Chris had had a taste for the high life. He'd get on a plane at the drop of a hat and whisk Trish off for long, romantic weekends. They ate out more often than they cooked and Chris had a garage full of golf clubs, fishing rods and expensive road bikes. But since the children he'd had to look for simpler pursuits, a hobby which didn't require a great deal of equipment or preparation and preferably one he could do in his lunch break at work. Running had been Trish's idea, insisting the fresh air and exercise would do him and his waistline good. He didn't have the natural physique for it, but the exertion fired him up and so now he couldn't imagine a day going by when he didn't get out for at least half an hour.

Today though was a little different, today was Chris Wilson's first competitive event and whilst it was only a fun run he was already starting to buckle under the burden of expectation.

***

'Black and two, just how you like it,' Michael Healy said passing the insulated cup through the open window, 'They're fresh out of croissants.'

'Already?' Bennett shot Healy a look.

'Already.'

'Fuckin' 'ell, Mike. One thing.'

He let it go, again.

'Got you a Danish instead.'

A small peace offering never went amiss, especially as Healy had a feeling that he and Bennett were going to be spending a lot of time together today. The assignment they'd pulled had developed quite a reputation through the service, viewed by the career minded and energetic as a punishment and by the older, slower operatives as a chance to catch up on some much needed rest. The most excitement it had ever produced had been the previous week when Bennett and Healy had unexpectedly been told to take the day off. That had been well received. They'd gone for lunch and a couple of pints together in The Goat on Kensington High Street before heading home early.

As Healy opened the passenger door to get in he glanced up the tiny row of townhouses to the Merc. parked less than a hundred yards away. It did him good to feel there were a couple of guys, in a car very much like their own just a few yards up the road, having an equally shitty time. Healy straightened his jacket, hitched up his trousers and sat down.

The problem with this job, Healy thought as he stared past his own reflection, was that most of the time you were either scared shit-less or bored shit-less and just now, listening to Bob Bennett slurping his coffee and droning on about nothing in particular, it was definitely the latter. Bennett and Healy had worked together on and off for ten years. They'd first paired up in 2001 when the war on terror had been declared. Initially the two men had got along rather well. Operations had been, by and large, successful, and when not working together they bought each other pastries and coffee in the mornings and pints of real ale at the Vauxhall Tavern near the river in the evenings. Then, quite suddenly their relationship had soured, but when asked by their respective partners neither could say exactly why. There had been no one particular incident. Perhaps they had simply spent too much time in each other's company? Perhaps it was Bennett's insistence on calling Michael, Mike, in that over familiar knock about way which Michael had always detested but never bothered to correct? Perhaps it was the age difference? Bennett, at fifty, and ten years Healy's senior was already starting to contemplate retirement. Either way they had endured a bad couple of years. They'd hardly spoken except when called upon to, tolerating each other but little more. Then Healy had settled down and started a family and tensions had eased considerably. Bennett's wife had sent him to work with freshly knitted booties and a bonnet for their first born and the resultant embarrassing exchanging of such feminine gifts had done much to re-build broken bridges.

Hunter's head was pounding. There was a chink in the curtains and a shaft of early morning light was catching him. He screwed up his eyes against the sun and shifted his head. He'd had an extraordinarily uncomfortable night even by his standards, but thanks to the whisky had achieved a sleep of sorts. Perhaps if he could just get the light from his eyes he might manage a little more. He twisted awkwardly on his makeshift bed. Then he heard a click. A very quiet click. It took some time for the sound to register. The sound of a front door closing. He half went back to sleep and was barely aware of the building's main door opening and shutting. The light caught him again and finally he gave up and knelt on the floor next to the sofa.

Amy had gone.

Fighting back the nausea and the splitting headache Hunter looked for his shoes. He sat unsteadily on the edge of the Chesterfield and struggled to put on his desert boots. Where the hell was she off to?

There was a polite tap at the living room door and George Wiseman shuffled in. It was early but he was washed, shaved and dressed.

'Good morning.'

'She's gone.'

Wiseman stared back at him blankly.

'Amy. She's gone.'

'When?'

'Just now, I think. I'm not sure, I was asleep.'

Wiseman was at the window atypically throwing back the curtains.

'Well, there's no sign of her outside. We need to find her and quickly.'

'Shit.'

'Stay calm, Scott. I think there may be help at hand.'

'Help?' Hunter couldn't imagine what the old boy was talking about.

'There are two gentlemen outside who may well be able to assist us.'

'Outside?'

'Yes, in a black car,' George craned forward to get a better look. 'They appear to be taking their breakfast.'

'The Audi, PVG34HG?' Hunter asked, still struggling with a disobedient shoelace.

'How could you possibly know that?'

Hunter shrugged. 'Shanghai International and the chemical symbol for mercury. The numbers come more easily.'

'Do they?'

'Sure,' Hunter said rubbing his forehead and barely looking up. 'The other car, is that still there, the Merc, 248X465?'

'Yes, yes it is,' Wiseman replied, squinting to read the plate.

'That one was easy. One hundred and fifteen thousand three hundred and twenty.'

'I'm sorry young man, I haven't the faintest idea what you are talking about.'

'The number of positive commandments in The Torah multiplied by Mozart's Dissonance Quartet. One hundred and fifteen thousand three hundred and twenty.'

'Of course it is.' Wiseman said, noting with a degree of satisfaction that Hunter was still unable to tie his shoelace.

'But I still don't see how they're going to be able to help us?'

'Because Scott, the men sitting in that car work for the British Secret Service. And those,' he gestured dismissively towards the blacked out Mercedes, 'unless I am very much mistaken, the Russian. They, or people very much like them have been parked outside this flat for the last twenty years. The Americans never seemed too bothered.'

'So you are a spy?'

Wiseman's brow furrowed.

'Such an ugly little word,' he said.

'It's an ugly little profession, isn't it?'

'Shall we go and see if these fine upstanding young gentlemen who have sat so patiently for so long have anything to say about Amy's whereabouts? I think that, after twenty years it's about time I at least said hullo, don't you?'

Wiseman hesitated by the front door.

'You may find this of some use,' he said handing Hunter the cricket bat he'd first seen next to Wiseman's umbrella stand. 'Come along.'

Showing surprising agility for a man of his age, Wiseman bounded down the steps of his flat and stood next to the open window of the Audi A4, jabbing a tobacco stained finger across its bonnet for Hunter to do the same and stand by the opposite window.

Bob Bennett looked up, 'What the fuck do you think you're up to?' he spluttered, his mouth full of pastry.

'An extremely attractive young lady left this flat no more than a few minutes ago. You will have seen her. She is not the sort of young lady one forgets, if you follow me? All I should like to know is, where did she go?'

Bennett starred back with well-trained indifference. As a younger man he'd pounded the streets, so now he was quite happy for *Lost Persons* to be someone else's problem. Normally he'd have at least passed the time of day with the confused old pensioner, but the man standing next to him wasn't just any pensioner, he was the target, and early retirement or no, Bob Bennett knew the rules on interaction with the target even if they did initiate contact. Theirs was a watching brief. Keep stum. Don't get involved. 'No idea what you're talking about mate. Haven't seen anyone,' he lied, hoping he'd drawn a line under the matter, and returned to his Danish.

'I see.' Wiseman paused. 'May I just say how much I admire your necktie?'

What was he on about now? Bennett looked at the strip of burgundy silk snaking down his chest. It had been a birthday present from his wife, or had it been Christmas? he never could remember. He suspected she'd hurriedly picked it out for him in a department store. The only thing Bennett thought you could honestly say of the tie was that it was wholly unremarkable.

'A Windsor knot, or do you favour the Grantchester?' Wiseman continued.

'Fucked if I know.' Surely even Alperton couldn't consider that social discourse.

'Shame. You really ought to find out. Although it does seem you may be more of a Pratt man.'

'What?'

'Do you mind?'

Wiseman lent forward, pushing his head through the open window.

'What the hell do you think you're doing?' Bennett balled at him.

'I'm sorry. You're going to have to speak up a little,' Wiseman said, touching his hearing aid, 'I'm a trifle deaf, you see?'

Bennett turned to Healey for help but Michael Healey was enjoying his partner's discomfort far too much to get involved. Wiseman reached into the car and took Bennett's tie in his hand, lifting it from his shirt to examine the knot. Before Bob Bennett could prevent him, and with his free hand, he pulled the tie through the steering wheel and out of the driver's window. Bennett's face was thrown violently forward and he cried out as scalding hot coffee splashed over his legs. Hunter glanced across the bonnet of the Audi, the purpose of the cricket bat now evident. Healy, the younger of the two men had started to open the passenger side door, now intent on aiding his colleague.

'Scott!' Wiseman barked at him.

Hunter struck the door with all the force he could muster. A satisfying dent appeared in the panel just below the handle and Healy swiftly retreated. Hunter repositioned himself and tried to stop shaking. Now Healy turned his attention to Bennett, trying to ease the choke that Wiseman was exerting, but the larger man's frame prevented him.

Wiseman bent his head level with the struggling driver's.

'Now listen to me you shit. I know exactly who you are and I know exactly who you work for.' Time to take the new ball, George. 'As a matter of fact, I know your boss rather well, as I'm sure you are only too aware. I do not want to have to relate the sorry tale of our meeting when he next offers me a disappointingly cheap glass of brandy at his club.' Wiseman braced his knee against the car and drew the tie tighter, grinding Bennett's face painfully against the steering wheel. 'So, I am going to ask you one last time before I break your jaw.'

'George!' Hunter was shouting at him from across the car.

'A young lady left my flat some minutes ago. She has long dark hair and is a little taller than me.'

'George!'

'All I want to know is, in which direction did she go? It really is terribly simple.'

'George, for Christ's sake.'

Wiseman looked up, never loosening his grip on Bennett's tie. At the corner of the street, just by the café, stood Amy, a newspaper in one hand, a takeaway coffee in the other.

'She's there George. For Christ's sake let him go.'

Seeing them, Amy raised the paper and waved. George let his grip relax and Bennett snapped his head back.

'You crazy old bastard,' he shouted 'Alperton'll hear about this.' He tugged at the knot, unable to loosen it. The electric window went up and before Wiseman could move from the road the Audi roared to life and screeched off at speed.

'Bloody Hell, George, what were you thinking?'

The attack had taken its toll on the old man and Hunter put an arm around Wiseman's shoulder as they watched Amy walk towards them. He started to laugh, shaking with the relief and then Wiseman was laughing too.

'I've been wanting to do that for a hell of a long time,' the old man smirked.

'*I'm going to ask you once more before I break your jaw?*' Hunter replied, doing his best to ape Wiseman's cut glass accent.

'Don't forget young man, I've worked in Hollywood.'

They watched Amy approach a junction. She was nearly with them. She stepped off the kerb to avoid a bollard on the pavement and a badly parked car, but before either of them could react the car's door swung open and the hulking figure Hunter had last seen leaving his house on Danforth Road emerged. One huge arm grabbed Amy around her slender waist whilst the other jabbed something into the side of her neck. She went limp almost immediately, never given a chance to struggle. With barely any effort the giant threw her into the back of the car. A moment later and he was in the driver's seat, gunning the engine.

Hunter raced up the road, but it was all over by the time he reached the junction and the freshly painted bollard. He caught sight of the car one final time as it turned by the café and was lost in London's traffic. Hunter had the same desperate feeling he'd experienced twenty-four hours earlier upon discovering Joth's lifeless body. His ears began to hum with the sound of his own blood, his body limp and useless, a deep cold spreading to the very tips of his fingers, whilst a clammy sweat coated his brow. He turned and without knowing where he was going, walked back towards 24 Lansdowne Terrace.

'Scott.' A voice though near, sounding from afar. It was Wiseman, 'Scott, I'm sorry. We really must go inside.'

'I've got to find her,' Hunter mumbled.

'Of course we do, but in my experience we will need to be inside and near a telephone. Now come along.'

They stood either side of George's antiquated telephone like a pair of expectant fathers. Hunter hadn't given his mobile a thought for the previous twenty-four hours but now was inspecting it with a degree of horror. Twelve missed calls. It had remained on silent since he'd crept past Joth's body. There were voicemails from the university, a text from Alec checking he was okay and most chillingly a message from the police asking him to contact them with the utmost urgency. He switched the iPhone's ringer back on. The battery life was down to an unhealthy thirty percent.

Moments later it was this phone which rang and not Wiseman's. He placed it on the table by the old man's typewriter and turned on the speaker. An ugly electronic voice filled the room.

'Now we both have something which belongs to the other. Bring the list to the statue of Peter Pan in Hyde Park at twelve o'clock. He knows the place. Bring the list and the girl goes unharmed.'

George nodded, but before Hunter could reply, confirm that he understood the arrangements or ask if Amy was all right, the line went dead.

He slumped into Wiseman's armchair. The magnitude of what had happened only now hitting him. Who was this person who seemed so intent of hurting everyone close to him and why were they doing it? What was the nature of the list? He turned on George Wiseman.

'We're going to need some sort of plan, but first, you're going to tell me about the names on that list.'

'I can't.'

'You can't or you won't?' Hunter rubbed his hands across his face. He was desperately tired and in need of a shave. 'You know the people on that list. You've always known. And if I'm to help Amy I need to know too. So?'

'That's not how it works, Scott.' Time for some good honest line and length, George. 'First we were never told. We were given the information to encode, that was all. Only one person ever knew the whole story and I'm afraid I'm not that person. So, whilst I may recognise those names, they are nothing more than that to me. Names.' A touch of wristy spin at the end perhaps, but on the whole largely wicket to wicket stuff.

'And secondly,'

'We aren't going to be at the Peter Pan Monument at twelve o'clock.'

'What?'

'We're not going to give him the list. I'm sorry Scott, I can't let you.'

'That's not your decision to make. I'm getting Amy back. You can tag along if you like.'

'Scott, this man is a killer. He won't hesitate to use violence. If we do as he asks there is no reason for me to believe that he will not try to kill all three of us. We cannot go.'

Hunter tapped the shoulder bag cradled on his knee.

'That's not for you to say. I'm going. I'll take my chances.'

'I admire your sense of chivalry Scott, but listen to yourself. This isn't your world.'

'Perhaps, but it is yours, isn't it?' The old man choose not to hear him. 'Isn't it?'

'You're an academic. A good one I'm sure, but you're not a...'

'A spy? Like you?'

'If you want to take this man on you had better use the skills *you* possess. You'll never beat him in a street fight. Don't forget he's armed.'

'What would you do then?'

Now's the time to dig in, George. Play the long game, think of the second innings and try not to lose a wicket cheaply before tea.

'First you must send the list to someone you trust. I mean *really* trust.'

'Professor Sinclair?'

'The founder of your little "club"? Too obvious, he'd be the first place I'd look.'

'Lazarus.'

'The diseased beggar? Lazarus? Who the hell is Lazarus?'

'He's part of our...' Hunter was reluctant to use the word again. 'He breaks Enigma codes. He's a friend, although I've only ever met him online. I couldn't tell you where he lives.'

'No.'

'But surely he'd be ideal?'

'No. Not a ghost. Someone you know and trust.'

'Alec then. He's my oldest friend. He knows codes better than I do and he'd do anything for Amy.'

'And you really trust him?'

'Yes.'

'Alec it is then.'

'I'll email it all to him, but leave it in the original code. He should have my copy of the algorithm by now. He's not stupid, he'll work it out.'

'There is one small problem. As you can see,' George gestured towards his aged Olivetti, 'I have yet to embrace email or the horrors of the World Wide Web.'

Hunter smiled. 'Leave that to me.'

He opened up the MacBook and let it search for wireless routers. The many adjacent houses and flats threw up an impressive array of machines but they were all password protected. It was the work of seconds for Hunter to fire up a short programme which began capturing packets from each of the strongest WEP addresses. Another programme cracked the packets and provided the users passwords and details. He was in.

'I'm impressed Mr. Hunter.'

'I shouldn't be. It's pretty straight forward stuff really, we just leech off someone else's broadband.'

Hunter composed a brief email asking for Alec's help, wrote in the Lorenz code with no further explanation and pressed send.

'Now, how are we going to get Amy back?'

7

Hunter had watched Joth take money from his bank's hole in the wall on enough occasions to easily remember his pin number, 1789, the birthyear of his dead friend's Germanic hero. The old man had said that they shouldn't suppose the rendezvous would be straight forward, simply handing over the material and expecting to have Amy returned wouldn't be enough. He'd cautioned Hunter that an insurance policy of sorts wasn't just advisable, it was essential. The camera though had been Hunter's idea, but when he'd looked to the old boy, Wiseman had shaken his head, closed his eyes and let out an involuntary grunt, Hunter presumed at the futility of their situation.

"I really have all the photographs I need," he'd said gesturing towards the crowded piano lid and reaching for his cigar holder, and so Hunter had caught the first available tube to Tottenham Court Road, but not before Wiseman had insisted he tell him exactly what he intended to do. He made Hunter walk him through every step of his plan and then, once he'd sanctioned it, the old boy made him prepare another plan altogether in case anything should go wrong. Then he had helped Hunter work out an escape route.

The counter was awkwardly situated as Wiseman had suggested it should be. The man who owned the shop, McAllister judging by the broadly painted sign outside, eyed Hunter suspiciously from the moment he entered. McAllister's Photographic was the third shop he'd scouted on Tottenham Court Road. The first hadn't sold quite what he was after, the second, an Indian run enterprise had been far too busy and Hunter had worried about becoming trapped if anything should go wrong, but in McAllister's there was just the one man running the shop. Hunter guessed he was in his late forties, his hair was deserting him and he awkwardly carried a little too much weight, a slim line of perspiration running unerringly down the back of his pale blue shirt. He quickly acknowledged Hunter with a perfunctory nod before returning to a stock order which was refusing to tally. McAllister fitted Hunter's requirements perfectly and so he got to work choosing from the array of high end SLRs on display. Any one of the top end bodies would do but he plumped for a Cannon. It was the lens which most concerned him, a telephoto with the highest zoom available. Next an 8 gigabyte memory card and finally a monopole on which to rest the heavy lens and camera.

Hunter waited for the shop's only other customer to leave and nervously approached the owner. He placed the items on the counter and tried to look as confident in front of the man he assumed to be McAllister as he could. McAllister rang everything through the till without comment before placing each item into a large branded plastic bag. Hunter found Joth's wallet and McAllister offered him the machine. He keyed in the four digits he'd seen his dead friend use so often and waited anxiously whilst the owner regarded the card machine's display, then there was an intrusive beep and paper was spewing out of the back of the card reader.

'We've had a few problems recently,' McAllister commented as he tore off the rejected receipt, reset the machine and handed it back to Hunter, who was certain he'd keyed in the correct pin number. Now there was the very real possibility that, following the events of the previous day, Joth's card had been cancelled. Hunter would wait and see if McAllister's machine would co-operate and if it refused he would be forced to resort to Wiseman's plan B.

Once again, a significant tail of paper rolled out of the rear of the card machine but this time when McAllister addressed him much of the Dundonian's earlier *bonhomie* had disappeared.

'Rejected again, son.'

'Would you mind very much if I used your phone. I'm sure I can sort this out with one quick call to the bank,' Hunter replied as casually as he felt able.

When McAllister turned his sweaty back on Hunter to retrieve his telephone from beneath the counter, Hunter bolted. He grabbed at the bag and ran as hard as he could towards the door, hoping to take the Scotsman, who would still have to navigate the difficult counter, by surprise. Hunter sprinted from the shop, turning sharply, barely registering the blacked-out BMW parked on the opposite side of the street and continued up Tottenham Court Road and away from the tube station. This wasn't the first time someone had tried to rip McAllister off and throwing the phone uselessly to the floor he was quickly after Hunter, shouting to a pair of policemen patrolling further up the street.

A quick look to his right and Hunter found what he had been searching for. Mindful of the large plastic bag full of photographic equipment at his side he vaulted a safety barrier running along the curb and began weaving in and out of the oncoming cars. As he reached the traffic calming island in the centre of the road and the vans and taxis around him changed direction Hunter heard what he took to be two sets of heavy police boots land behind him, but there was no time to turn and see, he must press on. The police would have leapt the barrier as he had. He was just one lane of traffic away from safety as two cars shot past, the second blasting its horn as it swerved to avoid him. Hunter sprinted across the road, cleared the barrier on the opposite kerb and scampered breathlessly down an alleyway running along the side of one of Central London's shabbier hotels. Halfway down the alleyway, in a neat line which belied the quality of the establishment, a row of industrial sized council bins. Hunter ignored the first two. The third stood invitingly open. He threw in the bag and slammed the heavy lid shut. Past the giant bins, a fire door kept ajar with half a house brick. He kicked the brick away before disappearing into the hotel, turning quickly to observe the heavily sprung door swing shut behind him.

An hour before entering the camera shop Hunter had scouted the area. Wiseman had suggested the plan. He had found the hotel and slipped in on the stern of a large group of young American backpackers. As they had swamped the concierge's tiny desk Hunter had quietly crept away. A long service corridor, lined with faded wallpaper from a different era, and a heavily worn and discoloured carpet, lead Hunter to the exit. He'd left a supermarket shopping bag tucked behind a fire extinguisher, opened the door, confident that any alarm had probably long since have been disconnected, found the half brick doorstop and opened the bin all before returning to Tottenham Court Road.

Steadying his breath Hunter recovered the flimsy plastic bag and pulled out Wiseman's overcoat and a floppy cricket hat he had spotted in his hallway. With the brim of Wiseman's hat pulled down shielding his face and the party of American tourists still checking in, he left the hotel, crossed the street and watched as the two policemen exited the alleyway. He saw one of the men check the first of the bins and then his partner was calling him away as his walkie-talkie crackled to life with more urgent matters. He would wait a while longer before gathering his spoils.

***

Hunter sensed they were running out of time. He found a large oak with one low branch between them and the Peter Pan Monument. The branch obscured him nicely and was not so high that with the monopole he couldn't get a good shot of the area. He flicked the switch to manual, f numbers and shutter speeds an unwelcome liability, then put the Cannon's view finder to his eye and, ignoring the preening ducks and distant swans, rattled off a swift sequence of photographs; empty benches, overflowing rubbish bins and a close up of the boy who never grew old. Then, adjusting the telephoto lens, Hunter found a corner of the envelope Wiseman had taped under the bench. There was still no sign of Amy.

'He isn't coming, is he?'

'He'll be here,' Wiseman said, pushing back a heavy French cuff to examine his watch.

The lead runners were just starting to appear. Hunter tracked a willowy athlete as he pounded past the statue. Not far behind him, a trailing pack. They seemed fresher than the leader and Hunter supposed they were bidding their time before moving in for the kill.

'What is this?' Wiseman was asking.

'A fun run.'

'Really, do such things exist? Surely to god no one runs for fun, only for purpose.'

'You'd be surprised, George.' Hunter looked anxiously at the envelope. This had never been part of the agreement. This had been Wiseman's idea and Hunter was praying to god that it worked. There was still no sign of the giant who had carried Amy off. The old man stood next to him, shaded from the midday sun by the overhanging tree. Hunter watched as a group of runners lolloped past and then flicked back to keep an eye on the envelope. They'd agreed not to confront the giant, banking on him phoning Hunter on his mobile when they didn't show up at midday. Hunter had had to admit, the old man did seem to know what he was doing.

'He's not coming. Where is he?'

'Scott, he'll be here.' Wiseman gave Hunter's arm a reassuring tap and then checked his watch again.

'Then why do you keep doing that? You're making me nervous.'

'He'll be here.' The old man nodded grimly. 'It's time.'

***

Chris Wilson was setting a good pace. A clear getaway had helped. At Marble Arch he'd met some of the other runners and his nerves had started to settle down. Andrew had come down from Glasgow the night before and Stewart was another Londoner, the three falling into nervous conversation whilst going through their warm ups. They'd listened distractedly to a minor TV celebrity needlessly shower them with incoherent words of encouragement before sounding a klaxon and sending them on their way. The trio tracked each other around most of the course until, just before the 10k mark, Chris had started to tire and let the other two press on without him. He checked his running computer. Not a bad effort, and there had been television cameras at the start, so always the chance that Ben and Sophie would see their dad after all.

***

Hunter scoured the surrounding area for any sign of Amy or her abductor. The runners were pouring past in ever increasing numbers, a bewildering array of shapes and sizes, styles and motivations. And then he saw her, her hair, her long, dark, beautiful hair, uncharacteristically messy and lank. The telephoto zoomed in close, the camera steady on its monopole. He could see her clearly now. She looked terrible, her eyes puffy, her face drawn and tired. Even the pearls around her neck seemed to have lost their glister. Over her shoulders a silver heat sheet and next to her, obligingly supporting her, the giant with the shaven head. He wore a red tracksuit and running shoes and for the first time Hunter glimpsed a strange swirl of tattoo which bled out from under the tracksuit top and up towards his ear, covering his neck. Wedging the monopole against his foot he zoomed in close on the man and then pulled back to include Amy. Whichever drug the giant had used appeared still to be at work, her movements laboured and lethargic. Hunter felt she was struggling simply to place one foot in front of the other, looking ready to stumble at any moment, but then the tracksuited monster at her elbow grabbed her more firmly and Hunter caught another flash of silver as his hand pulled Amy to him. The giant helped her to the bench where she collapsed, gratefully lolling to one side. Hunter continued to record events as the kidnapper scanned the area, whilst regularly checking his watch. He didn't leave it long after the appointed time before producing a mobile phone from a zipped tracksuit pocket. He fiddled with it a while, checked his hostage and then, as they had anticipated he would, called Hunter's phone. The same ugly disguised voice.

'This was not the arrangement. I have the girl. Where is it?'

'Under the bench.'

Realising that he was being observed the giant looked around, then quickly ducked down and retrieved the envelope. Hunter recorded every moment onto the Cannon's memory card. The giant, cradling the mobile under his chin, ripped open the envelope and withdrew two sheets of paper; the original code which had arrived so mysteriously on Hunter's doorstep just days before and the decoded list of names, *en clair*. He inspected both quickly, folded the sheets and thrust them into his top before taking up the phone again.

'This is not what we agreed. Where is the list?'

'You have them. Now let her go.'

'No. Where is it?'

'You *have* it. I'm watching you, now let her go.'

The giant was inspecting the surrounding parkland, straining to locate them.

'This is not the list. Another list. Don't play games with me boy.'

Hunter didn't know what to think and he couldn't believe what he was hearing. George Wiseman was looking expectantly at him and so he mouthed "other list".

Nothing.

Perhaps the deaf old boy couldn't make him out. 'What other list?' he shouted, his hand over the receiver.

The old man certainly heard that. His eyes fell to the ground and his shoulders sank, caught cheaply at the boundary waving lazily at the loose ball. He turned to face Hunter, and in that moment, as Wiseman's tired watery eyes met his, Hunter knew. He knew everything and nothing. He knew something was terribly wrong. Their plan, such as it had been, was falling to pieces.

'For Christ's sake George,' Hunter hissed at him, 'what other list?'

Wiseman's face filled with the sorrows of a lifetime.

'I'm sorry, Scott,' he said quietly letting his gaze return to the park floor. Then Hunter watched horrified as Wiseman turned and slowly walked away.

The giant had been clever to suggest this spot on this particular day. As Hunter tried frantically to find Amy in his viewfinder, he cursed George Wiseman. He'd been a fool to trust him. He struggled frantically with the heavy lens to try to recapture her. Runners. There were runners everywhere. Hunter forced himself to slow down, to steady his breathing and remain calm. With the naked eye he could see her sat on the bench, the silver aluminium heat sheet around her shoulders. The giant seemed to have disappeared into the crowd. Hunter trained the camera on the bench and put it to his eye.

At first glance Amy looked as she had done just moments before, but then he watched as her body crumpled and slumped forward, a small patch of red spreading across her stomach.

'No!'

Hunter was up and running towards the lake, the monument and Amy, screaming at the top of his voice, the camera long forgotten and discarded. The man in the red tracksuit had been moving away, blending in with the sea of athletes around him, but when he heard Hunter's shouts he turned and in the same movement withdrew the silenced Glock from his tracksuit top. Hunter was running straight towards him, unable to think of anything other than Amy. The giant steadied himself and there was a quiet puff. Hunter felt the air ripple as a bullet whistled past him. The giant advanced, knelt, adopted a firing position, bracing himself against the black railings surrounding the lake and shot again. People were screaming now and scattering wildly. If Hunter continued to run towards the armed man there would be only one outcome and then he would never save Amy. The Serpentine separated them, that had always been the plan. If he were to help her he had to stay alive and find a way around the water, but first he had to find cover. In the distance he saw George Wiseman slowly leaving the park.

Hunter had chosen the spot because there was clear open water between the oak tree and the monument, but now his carefully chosen location's advantages would be the very thing which got him killed. He was running away from the old oak, and out into the open, leaving the only available cover behind him. The harder he ran the more likely he was to be shot. He would have to turn around and head back to the safety of the oak tree. As he span around he saw the giant cradling the pistol in one huge steady hand. Hunter started to weave and dodge. He knew if he ran straight to the tree there would be only one outcome.

As he grabbed his messenger bag a third shot thudded into the tree next to him. He threw the bag's shoulder strap around his neck, picked up the camera by its monopole and ran. Banking that the gunman would think he had headed south, following Wiseman to the safety of the road, the bridge and the promise of heavily populated museums, Hunter instead swung sharply left and sprinted North towards the Italian Gardens and Lancaster Gate. The trees lining the east side of the lake provided some cover and praying that the giant hadn't seen him, Hunter pressed north towards the Bayswater Road. If he could just make it to Lancaster Gate, then there was a chance. The shoulder bag was an encumbrance and the camera was probably slowing him down too but he had to have them. They were evidence. If he could stay alive long enough he would need them, he would need them to catch the man who had killed Joth and Amy. Hunter ran. Briefly he lost sight of his attacker as he pounded up the track. He looked over at the heavy foliage on the opposite bank of The Serpentine. His attacker, Amy's attacker, had disappeared behind a mixture of thick old trees and wild blackberry bushes. Hunter broke cover, running out from behind a gnarled and long dead tree to the marble safety of the Italian fountains. The ground in front of him leapt and kicked as a bullet barely missed him. He didn't know where to head next. As he reached Jenner's thoughtful statue he saw the exit to the park. Hunter vaulted the thick railings, colliding with an entirely unlovely council litter bin, sending him staggering to his knees.

Chris Wilson stood at the rally point in the Italian Gardens wrapped in a heat seet, basking in the adoration of his wife and children. He'd completed his first 10k run. His time had been slower than he'd have liked, but his kids weren't to know that. Ben leapt into his arms and he hadn't been able to dislodge Sophie from his leg since finishing. Trish had kissed him with genuine pride and he was enjoying his fifteen minutes of fame, around his neck a medal to show that he had taken part.

Suddenly, out of the corner of his eye he was aware of a commotion. There was a lot of shouting and screaming, but there always was at these events. Then he saw the young man racing towards them, a wild terrified look in his eye, frantically waving his arms for them to get out of his way. The Wilson family looked at him, shocked by his appearance. Certainly not a competitor from his attire. A freelance photographer perhaps? In the split second it took them to process the information the bullet struck Chris Wilson's leg, shattering his left femur and sending him to the ground. He would never run again.

Hunter saw the man drop. He heard him cry out. He wanted to stop, to help, but he had to keep going. He was at the rallying point, tables groaning with sports drinks and branded health bars. He was responsible. He was bringing this armed man into their midst. Another innocent person had been hurt, or worse, because of him, and still he had no answers. There were competitors everywhere.

Some on the fringes had looked across at him or the fallen runner and now like a wave, the realisation that something was terribly wrong, began to spread. They started to panic. Slowly at first, but then with a terrifying speed. New acquaintances who only moments before had been exchanging phone numbers, swapping email addresses and posing for selfies, were now trampling over each other in their panic to get away from the shooter. Hunter could hear children screaming for their parents, women crying, athletes only moments before too tired to move, running once more. Hunter wondered if he could afford another look over his shoulder. He easily vaulted a short row of box hedge, before clearing a marble wall. He was amongst the fountains now and heading towards the old pump house and Lancaster Gate. He flicked his head round quickly. The giant was nowhere to be seen. Had he lost him? Had he given up? Hunter stopped to turn properly. Now he could see him. He was emerging from the opposite side of the gardens, briefly obscured by a huge Victorian urn. He was further back than Hunter had expected. Perhaps he had been distracted by the large numbers of people? Perhaps he was worried someone would confront him? Surely there must be police at such a huge event? He seemed preoccupied. Christ, Hunter realised, he was reloading. If he took the path the giant would gun him down for sure. Two fountains stood between him and the slope which would take him from the park and away from the people. Summoning all his strength he ran straight for the nearest fountain, leaping into the freezing water and immediately slipping on the bottom, his feet tangling in roots and tripping over pipes, his body shocked from the cold, but relieved to have dropped by a couple of feet and out of the gunman's eyeline. The freezing water was up to his chest but he had found some more cover behind a tall bank of reeds. A moment to catch his breath and assess the situation. He must press on, he must get out of the park. As he crawled from the first fountain he looked up at the pump building. If he went in there he would almost certainly be trapped. Another bullet cracked into the building's 150-year-old façade. He had to get to the tube station. The shortest route should have been the quickest but now his black jeans and desert boots were heavy with water. Behind him another bullet cracked into the Carrara marble and then more screams. If he waded across the second fountain the giant would surely be on top of him. Once he'd been identified as the gunman's target everyone in front of him scattered, falling over each other in their desperation to get out of his way. Then he was at the steps to the old pump house. He clattered into a table, sending papers and empty drinks bottles flying. Keep going, he had to keep going. Hunter's muscles were burning as he pounded up the slope and out of the park.

He'd reached the Bayswater Road. Ahead the pedestrian crossing had just finished counting down and now London's traffic was running determinedly past again. To the right a bus stop, then diagonally opposite, on the other side of the road, Lancaster Gate Underground Station and where he supposed the giant would assume he was headed. So again, Hunter decided to try and shake him off by taking the less obvious route. And anyway, could he really bring this monster into a crowded tube station? He'd already killed Joth and probably Amy. He'd shot an innocent bystander in the leg. There had to be another way to lose him. If he could only put some distance between the two of them, but his sodden clothes were slowing him down, leaving an incriminating trail behind him. A taxi tore past and Hunter tried desperately to flag it down, but no taxi was going to stop for a soaking wet student. He would have to negotiate the Bayswater Road. He stumbled off the pavement. With everyone he cared about gone there was an overwhelming temptation to give up. If he stayed where he was either the London traffic or the gunman would finish him. Simpler then to just end it all and concede defeat, but something drove him on. Was there really a second list? Wiseman's actions certainly seemed to suggest so. Hunter had to keep going. He needed to know, now more than ever. He had to find that list.

His side of the road split into three lanes, two heading North, taking buses to the zoo and Marylebone Station, the third, and the one into which Hunter had stumbled headed West, hugging the top edge of the park. Before he'd gone more than two steps a 94 to Acton almost winged him, sending him scuttling back towards Hyde Park and danger. But then, in the distance, a line of red buses, each, if Hunter understood correctly, heading North. If he could manage a lane of traffic and position himself on the far side of one of the approaching buses that might buy him some time. Another car swerved past him sounding its horn and Hunter dragged himself onto the traffic island in the centre of the road. He turned in time to see his pursuer emerge from the park. Hunter ran, with no thought for himself or for the cars on either side of him. As he reached the pavement opposite the bullet struck. The 9 millimetre came from behind him and to his left, where his shoulder bag hung. It flattened him, knocking the air from his lungs, sending him sprawling to the ground. His hands reaching instinctively to brace his fall. Hunter felt the skin ripping from his palms as he skidded along the pavement, the camera on its monopole sliding away in front of him. One look at his shoulder bag told him its contents had probably saved his life, but that could all be for nothing. Was this it? Was this really where he was going to die, on an anonymous street corner in Central London? The passengers on board the 94 saw only a young man fall to the pavement and struggle to get up, any sound made by the silenced pistol drowned out by earphones and the onset of rush hour. Only a week before, on the same route, passengers on a similar bus had watched dispassionately as a woman had attacked her boyfriend with a stilettoed heel. It was just London. The bus moved on.

The giant was at the road now. He levelled the gun as Hunter struggled on the ground, the steady flow of traffic the only thing preventing him from pulling the trigger and finishing it.

Hunter scrambled to get to his feet but his legs wouldn't hold him, all his strength gone. The first of the buses approached the junction of the A402 where it began slowly to turn before heading north. He had to move now. The camera. He crawled the short distance to where the monopole lay. Ignoring the pain Hunter took it firmly in his hand and using it as a crutch, tried one tentative step followed by another. The second bus passed him. His cover was driving away. He needed to be up and moving before the third bus turned north otherwise it would be over.

As the last of the buses swept past on its way to North London Hunter tracked alongside, using the monopole as a cane. Gradually he was regaining his mobility and starting to jog. His back was agony where the shoulder bag and its contents had stopped the bullet and his hands felt raw and bloody but slowly he was starting to run. He took one last look to judge the distance between him and his assailant. For the first time he saw the man clearly. His shaven head, the pale eyebrows above mean little eyes and then he raised the gun and Hunter turned and fled up Westbourne Terrace.

Another busy junction and he was at Sussex Gardens not knowing whether to turn left by the church or keep moving. The gardens themselves were of no use, just a dot of tranquillity where overworked Londoners took their lunch and where he would be easily picked off. Better to keep moving.

Westbourne Terrace was a never-ending row of white stucco tenements, chequerboard porches and off white colonnades, understated and fragile black numbers finely painted halfway up each pair of pillars unenthusiastically advertising the property's address. Hunter ran past one after another, their doors firmly shut, but then, in the distance one block caught his eye. A renovation project, its weary Regency lath and plaster guts ripped out and replaced, its once grand façade wreathed in humiliating scaffolding and panels of blue plastic mesh to stop over curious pigeons from intruding. Gone the carefully painted numbers, exchanged for a folded piece of card espousing that, once upon a time, this had been number 52. Set off the pavement an enormous generator covered with warning stickers and diligently supplying electricity to power tools and the alarm system protecting the precious scaffolding. Amongst the wooden walkways and pipes and much to Hunter's astonishment, signs of life. One balcony, still open, two potted trees guarding over its entrance, a banner advertising the builder's name and telephone number fluttering indifferently in the breeze.

On each external floor ladders secured to the next, creating a zig-zag of tired aluminium, and then, next to the ladders, a snake. A long and winding wooden rubbish chute hastily constructed and descending awkwardly from a fourth floor window into a skip sitting next to the gently humming generator. As Hunter looked up, past the fourth floor he saw, at the very top of the building, dangling precariously in space from the highest scaffolding pipe, a block and tackle, its rope twisting and untwisting with a mind of its own. He almost ran straight into a pair of barechested workmen who had finished emptying a wheelbarrow of cement dust and rubble into the skip and were gingerly guiding it back down a long narrow plank. The place was littered with hard hats, empty cigarette packets, tool belts, the day's red tops and discarded clothing, the air thick with fine white dust, stale smoke and the smell of hard work. Brooms, chicken wire and abandoned electrical cable lay in an untidy pile alongside signs warning of work overhead. Hunter shoved past a man carrying an angle grinder, through a makeshift entrance and into the body of the house. Off to the right was the first flat, its front door missing. Inside more power tools, ladders and work benches holding rotary saws and routers. Hunter assessed the room quickly, there was nowhere to hide. He shot up the first flight of stairs. From behind him he heard the giant arriving, threatening the men outside.

The next landing was the same. Planks covering the stairs to allow more wheel barrows to come and go. Hunter was running out of options. He reached the third floor. This had been where he had seen an occupied apartment. He beat on the door but it was futile. Even if there had been someone home, by the time they had come to the door the giant would be on him. He would have to continue on and up, there was nowhere else to go and Hunter was running out of time.

When he reached the fourth floor he realised why the ladders outside had come to such an abrupt halt. There were no stairs to the fifth and final floor. He was trapped. On the landing were two doors. The first was locked and probably a bathroom. The second opened into the master bedroom. There was nothing. The room was completely bare. No furniture, no carpets, most of the plaster was missing from two of the walls and light switches and power sockets hung from naked cables, unsupported and twisted. Hunter listened as heavy footsteps climbed the stairs. He'd reached the end of the line. He watched the tip of the silencer poke into the room and then the huge man followed.

'You little shit.'

Hunter had never heard his real voice. Before it had always been electronically disguised. There was an accent, quite a heavy one too, but Hunter couldn't place it. He was much more concerned with the gun which was being levelled at him. He edged back towards the large bay windows at the front of the house as the giant advanced upon him.

'Where's the list?'

'I told you. I gave you what I had. That's it. There is no other list. I don't know what you're talking about.'

'Do you think I'm fucking stupid? Give me the list,' he barked, waving the gun to emphasis his request.

'I can't. I can't give you what I don't have.'

'The camera.'

Hunter had forgotten he even had the camera. With shaking, bloodied hands he unclipped the Cannon from its mount.

'Slowly.'

He was about to relinquish his only piece of evidence. Once he'd given that away, then what? There would be nothing to stop the giant from killing him too. This might be his only chance. If he could catch the man off guard he might be able to buy enough time to get past him and down the stairs. He held the camera as firmly as his bloody right hand would allow and threw it with all his strength at the man's head. Its size and shape made it an awkward projectile and useless as a weapon. The giant deflected it easily then, disappointed by his adversary and shaking his head, picked up the camera and deftly removed the memory card, slipping it into his pocket.

'Don't get cute you little bastard,' he growled at Hunter before smashing the Cannon on the floor, sending shards of expensive plastic splintering across the room.

That was it. Hunter had played his last card, and lost. But he still held the monopole. As the giant advanced on him he carefully unclipped the telescopic leg and waited. He waited for the sparkling one liner, the witty *bon mot*, the Hollywood zinger that would surely be the last words he would ever hear and would have caused Amy to roll her eyes in incredulity. He waited for his final chance to hear the monster's true voice.

Nothing.

Hunter was pent against the open sash window, a fresh breeze playing along his back. The giant was three feet from him and repositioning the gun with only one intention. What was it the old man had said? *You'll never beat him in a street fight.* Well he hadn't been right about much up to now. Hunter was going to pray he'd been wrong about that too. He saw the sun glint off the ring on the man's left hand as it held the gun's rugged grip. Not a wedding ring after all, but a Hell's Angel's grinning silver skull. Hunter clenched the foot of the monopole tightly in both hands and aimed for the glistening target. As the giant drew breath, steadying himself before delivering the *coup de grâce*, Hunter swung hard. The telescopic leg with its weighty metal mount, shot out to its full extension, simultaneously catching the side of the gun and the man's left hand and in that instant shattering the metacarpal of his third finger. He screamed in pain, dropping the Glock, which clattered across the floor and came to rest in the doorway. The giant, nursing his hand and cursing, was after it. Hunter had one chance. He turned and leapt into the wooden rubble chute which snaked down the front of the building. The pain as his bruised back scrapped against the entrance to the chute was excruciating and blood from his hands left an incriminating trail on the recently painted crisp white window sill. He would have to brace his descent. If he fell from this height at best he could expect to break both ankles. His hands were raw from his fall on the Bayswater Road, so he used his feet to slow himself. From inside the room he could hear the giant cursing him and howling with pain.

Hunter had been so careful not to fall down the chute but now he wasn't moving at all. Straining his neck, he craned upwards. The strap of his messenger bag had caught around one of the vertical struts making up the chute's mouth. He'd bought the bag because it had been advertised as durable and tough but now he was praying that it would tear and release him. Shifting his position Hunter let the strap take his full weight and hoped that the stitching would finally fail.

Methodically the giant retrieved his gun and prepared to finish the job. Even using his weaker hand, at this range and in such a small space, he ought to hit his target. He spun, ready to fire. But the room was empty. There was no way his mark could have slipped past him unnoticed, the gun had come to rest next to the door. For a fleeting moment the giant almost felt pity for the boy who had caused him so much pain. He must have been so terrified he'd taken his own life, throwing himself from the window. But just as quickly the moment passed and, holding his shattered hand the giant marched over to where Hunter had stood, prepared to see his latest victim's broken body lying bent and lifeless on the pavement below. Naturally, he would have preferred a cleaner outcome. He took great pride in his work, but once they were dead, they were dead and that was an end to it. And then he saw the chute. Clever little shit. He thrust the Glock down the wooden opening and loosed off a couple of speculative rounds.

Hunter was lying on a grimy bed of cement and rubble as the bullets hit home sending puffs of fine brick dust into the air. Battered and bruised and slowed by his injuries he dragged himself from the skip, grey cement clinging in patches to his wet clothing. He grabbed a

162

black Lonsdale hoodie that one of the builders had carelessly discarded and threw it over his head, his shoulder bag in hand, its broken strap trailing happily behind him as he stood on the pavement and weighed up his position. Hunter didn't have much time. He could already hear police sirens heading his way. North, the way his pursuer might expect, or south and back towards Hyde Park and the Police?

Neither. On the opposite side of the road he spotted a basement flat down a narrow, wrought iron staircase. Providing he made it across the road in time he ought to be able to observe his attacker leaving. If he was too slow, he would be trapped at the bottom of a stairwell with no escape. Hunter dodged through the traffic and threw himself down the heavy metal steps.

A police car tore down Westbourne Terrace heading towards the park as Hunter's pursuer left, the man turning sharply and heading north as he had suspected he would. Hunter was finally able to catch his breath. He was finally able to take stock of recent events. He dropped the bag and broke down.

8

'Who is this?'

'Scott.'

Silence.

'She's dead George. He killed her. Right in front of us.' Hunter hadn't wanted to accept Amy's death but now the words came tumbling out.

'You must come here, to the flat I mean. I have something I need to show you,' Wiseman said sounding unnaturally calm.

'You're kidding, right? The police are everywhere.' Hunter hesitated. 'I should just go and turn myself in.'

'No, Scott. There are things you do not yet understand.'

'What things?'

'You *must* come to the flat. I have something to show you that will explain everything. It will explain everything about your grandfather.'

'My what?'

Silence.

'George?'

Hunter looked at his iPhone. He pressed the indented home button at the bottom of its screen. Dead. He swore under his breath. His grandfather? What the hell did his grandfather have to do with anything? Papa was in a retirement home in Somerset and had been for years. He'd been diagnosed with early onset dementia and Scott's father hadn't been able to take care of him. Hunter couldn't remember ever meeting his mother's father. If he was going to go to Wiseman's flat he would have to be extremely careful. He couldn't think how the police would have tied the old man into any of this, but then there were all his buddies from the secret service to worry about. He'd wait until after dark. Hunter pulled the hoodie tight over his head.

Lansdowne Terrace was quiet now, the café at the end of the road having long since closed for the day. Kensington's ladies had moved on first to wine bars and then theatres in the West End. Hunter decided to take his time approaching the flat. He had nothing to lose now. The old man wasn't going anywhere, but there was still the issue of two secret service cars, one British, one Russian. Hunter preferred to conduct his meeting with Wiseman on his own terms and that was going to involve encouraging these unwanted guests to leave. Nearest him, the Russian car with its diplomatic X plates. If his plan worked, he might kill two birds with one stone and remove the other car as well.

He observed the two cars for nearly an hour. The driver of the Merc. was a ferocious smoker finishing three cigarettes in that time. Hunter was waiting for the next butt to be thrown from the window. He edged forward. Through the semi-tinted windows he watched the flare of a lighter. Hunter had never been much of a smoker, but the guy in the car smoked with the urgency of need, then discarded the bulk of each cigarette, so he didn't have long to wait before the car's electric window came down a couple of inches and a largely unfinished butt joined the pile growing on the pavement. Hunter sprang up and alongside, but before he could even begin his well-rehearsed speech the uncompromising looking Muscovite inside pressed a button and the window whirred shut. For a fleeting second, their eye's met. Now the Russians knew someone was prowling around outside their car. Wiseman was always telling him it was a good idea to have a plan B.

Hunter marched confidently in front of the Mercedes and put his shoulder bag on its bonnet. Theatrically he removed a scrappy piece of paper and an old orange biro. He couldn't see the driver through the tint, but he stared at where he thought the man ought to be and began to write. He didn't spare the beautiful paintwork of the Mercedes, putting his full weight behind the pen. Then, when there was still no reaction from inside the car, Hunter took the piece of paper and placed it on the windscreen.

Alperton at Russian Embassy.

He had no idea who Alperton was but his note certainly had the desired effect. The engine sprang to life, the car was flung into gear and Hunter had to leap out of the way as it disappeared off and up Lansdowne Terrace, leaving the paper to flutter to the ground. No sooner had the Russians left than the lights of the A4 outside Wiseman's flat came on and that too disappeared, following the speeding Russians West at a discreet distance, presumably to find out where their counterparts were going in quite such a hurry. Hunter was free to approach the twelve steps leading to Wiseman's flat. He could see the main door was propped open, George's cricket bat keeping it ajar. Could the killer have come back? Needing something to defend himself with he picked up the bat, having long since abandoned the monopole. Inside the tiny close Wiseman's front door stood invitingly open. That was unlike the old man. Hunter tightened his grip on the weapon.

Music spilled from the kitchen. A transistor radio judging by the quality. Britten's Serenade. Not the original though, Hunter thought, listening for Pears's distinctively plaintive tone, no this must be a more recent recording. He'd never understood the professor's fascination with the piece, what took Britten and Blake twenty minutes to say Johnny Ramone could have done in two.

In the front room everything was as it had been. George, dressed in a flowing silk dressing gown, a decanter by his side, sat motionless before the empty fire. Only when Hunter moved further into the room, passed the piano and its photographic chronical did he realise something was very wrong. The old man's chin rested on his chest and there was the over powering smell of whisky and vomit. Wiseman's dappled hand dangled limply by his side, a tumbler lying relinquished on the floor, his naked feet exposing the hard, yellow claws of old age. Hunter saw prescription pill boxes on the table next to Wiseman's typewriter. George had taken his own life and so Hunter had no idea what made him do it, but he bent down and tried to find the old man's pulse. He wanted to close his eyes but couldn't.

This was the third dead body he'd seen in as many days; Joth, George and he felt he could now say, Amy. He took the decanter, poured what was left into a tumbler and found a space on the sofa which meant he didn't have to see Wiseman's body. The old man had said he would tell him something concerning his grandfather. Hunter grimaced. He wouldn't be telling him anything now, would he?

No, that wasn't quite true. Wiseman had said he'd *show* him something. Hunter got up and started searching the room, finally able to examine the books on Wiseman's shelves. An eclectic mix, from Albert Camus to Jean-Luc Godard, Hermann Hesse and Thomas Mann rubbing shoulders with Noam Chomsky and Ayn Rand but nothing which suggested a connection with Hunter's grandfather. From the books he moved to the photographs. Arranged on the mantlepiece just the collection of pictures one might expect of a dotting grandfather. Shots of babies, toddlers and then their first days at school. Again, nothing connecting Wiseman in any way with his grandparents. Perhaps the photographs on the piano would tell him more? These were from a different era, a black and white era, their absence of colour imbuing them with a sense of times long past and bygone days and much more in keeping with his grandparents. He saw the gala events, the sixties starlets and George proudly posing in his service uniform. That was certainly a time when his papa had been around, he'd seen similar photographs at his father's house. Hunter picked up the picture which had started it all. The picture on the dust cover of Wiseman's book, George in his black tie and dinner jacket, happily clutching a cigar.

He forced himself to examine Wiseman's body, what little of it there was. Hunter took a handkerchief and tried to tidy him up. He'd never appeared to be a large man but now he looked tiny, shrunken and pathetic, his skin although still warm to the touch, already starting to sallow and grey. His eyes which Hunter couldn't bare to shut seeming dull and glassy. Hunter looked over his shoulder towards the piano and its photographs. Photographs showing an energetic happy young man enjoying life. But that would not be the way *he* would remember him, a man who had taken such pride in his appearance, such delight in the finer things, no, Hunter would forever remember him as he was now. Awkwardly he padded him down, finding nothing, then finally he closed his eyes.

On the table by the window, where the Olivetti sat, were the tablets George had taken. A cocktail of oramorph and diazepam. Hunter knew enough to know they were painkillers, presumably for whatever illness had been slowly killing him. It was when he examined the pills that he saw the manuscript left next to the typewriter. Bound together with two colourful treasury tags it had been typed on the thinnest of paper.

A Life in Film, by George Wiseman

his address, and underneath in longhand;

For Scott. I am so very sorry. I made a terrible mistake.

So this was it? This was what the old man had insisted he return to the flat for? An unpublished manuscript detailing George's escapades in the film business? Hunter was struggling to imagine what that could possibly have to do with any of his grandparents. None of them had had anything to do with the film industry to the best of his knowledge. But this was certainly it. George's gift to him. Again he had the horrible feeling he was missing something. He flicked through the manuscript, the onion skin pages feeling false beneath his fingers, a poor imitation of the original, like one of Professor Sinclair's reproductions. Then, hearing police sirens from the other end of Lansdowne Terrace and fast coming to terms with his new life as a fugitive, Hunter slipped the manuscript into his bag. Taking one last look around the room he switched off the lights. The old man's kitchen was in front of him and so he guessed the room at the far end of the corridor must be the bathroom.

George's bathroom, whilst immaculate in almost every respect, had not been re-decorated in an extremely long time. The bath and sink were of a draconian brown plastic that, coupled with the lack of any natural light lent the room a gloomy, airless quality. Even Wiseman's clearly fastidious nature hadn't stopped a broadening limescale stain from developing beneath the bath's silver taps. Above the sink a faded plastic cabinet. Hunter regarded himself in its mirror. He looked exhausted but he knew that sleep would not come to him, not naturally. He opened the cabinet in the hope of finding something to bandage his hands with and tablets. Anything which might help him lose consciousness and escape the horrors of the waking world. Instead of Valium or Zolpidem, Hunter found nail scissors. He took a towel from the radiator and struggling with the small scissors, cut it into thin strips which he wound around his painful hands, then he began cutting off his hair. The old man had used cheap plastic disposable razors and so Hunter made a terrible mess of his head as he shaved it clean. It was as he was staring at his bald and bloodied reflection in the bathroom mirror that the whispering voices grew louder. He grabbed what remained of the hand towel and ran it over his bloodied head before rushing back into the sitting room. How could he have been so stupid, so unobservant? The photograph. George with his father. *Six* people in the background. *Six* names on the list. He turned the frame over. It had appeared quite an ordinary one, befitting an uninspiring group photograph. But now Hunter saw the silver hallmark. Wiseman didn't do drab. There was a wooden backplate with a supporting leg to stand the frame upon and along each side small silver clasps. Hunter undid them, removing the protective cover and placing it and the glass on top of the piano. He held the black and white photograph in his hands. On its reverse, written in elegant swirling script, the six names he had seen in code, plus the names of George and his father, Sam Wiseman and the date 1948. He turned the picture over and tried to put names to faces, but it was impossible. At least he knew when these people had lived and consequently he assumed that they were now probably all dead, the youngest of them looking to be in their thirties and one of the men considerably older than that.

Was there anything else to be learnt from the photograph? Their attire told him little, they were all wearing the same drab civilian clothing of post war Britain. The picture must have been taken in the late autumn or early winter of 1948, to one side a bare tree, its branches nakedly snaking into the cold clear sky, all of the subjects were heavily dressed, the men wearing long overcoats, some in hats and scarfs, the sole woman wearing a thick jacket and gloves. He'd always assumed it had been taken at Bletchley or at the very least somewhere in Britain. But most of the people, judging from their names, were German. Even Wiseman, Hunter supposed, might easily have been Weisman or Weissmann at one time. Was he now saying the photograph had been taken in Germany in 1948? It was possible but seemed unlikely and in any case hadn't it said Bletchley in George's book? But then Hunter was rapidly learning not to trust everything Wiseman had told him. Perhaps they were POWs who had decided to settle in Britain at the end of the war? That might be a simpler explanation. Hunter was sure he'd read that the last Germans had been repatriated as late as 1949. Another police siren echoed along Lansdowne Terrace from the busy main road as Hunter slipped the photograph into his messenger bag next to the manuscript and went to the window. The Audi was back. They must have returned whilst he'd been in the bathroom. He ran a hand over his poorly shaven head. The Russians had clearly had enough for one night and gone home. Hunter didn't have a home to go to but he couldn't stay in Wiseman's flat.

✳✳✳

Hunter recognised the man immediately. Christ these guys worked long hours. He tapped on the window and it came down. Hunter pulled off his hood and Michael Healy stared back. Perhaps, Healy mused, this job might turn out to be more interesting than he'd first thought.

'Remember me?' Hunter asked meeting Healy's curious stare. 'I need to talk.'

The two British field agents silently consulted one another and then the sound of the Audi's rear doors unlocking. Hunter climbed in and the doors locked behind him. He sat forward, his filthy elbows resting on immaculate front seats, his bloodied head pushed between Bennett's and Healy's.

'George is dead. Killed himself before you ask. Nothing to do with me. I'm going to need your help.'

Hunter spent the next half an hour in the blacked out Audi talking with Bennett and Healy. At the end of their meeting Bennett handed him a slip of paper. Hunter thanked him, pulled the hoodie tight over his head and left. He was going to have to find somewhere to sleep for the night.

9

David had contacted a specialists in Germany to find many of the parts. The company had swathed them in bubble wrap and painstakingly parcelled them in corrugated carboard and thick grey tape. After a somewhat convoluted journey across Europe the parts began to arrive in a steady trickle through the post, smothered in franking stamps and lurid fragile stickers.

The clock which lay in pieces on David's dining room table had originally been handcrafted by Anton Harder in Ransen near Frankfurt in 1883. Some people called them Torsion or Four Hundred Day Clocks, but to David it was the Anniversary Clock.

Harder had watched a servant lighting a chandelier. As the man lit each candle he'd turned the chandelier to light the next. Harder had realised that when the chandelier was released it would spin forward and back and he'd taken the idea and applied it to the pendulums in his clocks. Of course there were other stories too but David preferred this one. He reflected how upset Harder would have been to see one of his creations in such a condition. The glass bell had been so severely smashed he'd thrown it away and one of the brass finials was badly bent and twisted where the clock had landed. The torsion pendulum itself was delicate and whilst it appeared to the naked eye to be intact David knew it would need to be completely stripped, cleaned and reassembled and that that was going to be a fiddly and laborious task. Harder clocks were never the most accurate of time keepers but then David didn't care about that. For him it was a link to the past, not a way of measuring the present. He was painfully aware of where it had come from and the people it had belonged to. The clock, he rationalised, could not be held responsible for that, it was just a clock after all, a collection of cogs, springs and gears. He tried to conjure up images of the men and women who had wound and cared for the delicate timepiece. They were all dead now.

**

London at night becomes a different place to different people. It was 11 o'clock and many of the pubs around Trafalgar Square were still doing a brisk trade but now the streets were filling with the night's revellers, people streaming out of theatres and opera houses, restaurants and bars and each with their own separate agendas. Some hurrying to catch the last train home, others drunkenly falling into private hires, happy to worry about the cost, both physical and pecuniary, the following morning. The monied set who stayed in their wine bars, confident they could afford the cost of a black cab at any time. And amongst them all, the performers, the bar staff, the students who'd had too much and the stag and hen parties who'd had far too much.

Careful to avoid busy main roads and the possibility of being recognised by the police, Scott Hunter had walked to Trafalgar Square. He skirted three of London's most famous parks, drawn by the need to surround himself with the capital and its people, to disappear into their ranks, just another lost lonely soul on a muggy evening in May. On any other occasion he would have relished the warm spring air, but not this evening. Then, standing beneath Nelson's column looking south along Whitehall, amidst the partygoers and tourists the uncomfortable feelings of South Kensington returned. Landseer's bronze lions suddenly no longer protective and reassuring, but snarling and disloyal.

Hunter's clothes, such as they were, hung on him like rags, damp, torn and caked in cement dust, his shoes ruined. The paint splattered Lonsdale hoodie he'd found at the building site on Sussex Gardens now permanently covering his badly shaven head, the broken messenger bag held tightly in his bandaged hand. People were starting to stare at him, furtive glances exchanged between friends, colleagues, partners. Hunter couldn't afford to be recognised, not just yet. In the past forty-eight hours his life had been turned upside down. He looked at the young couples in Trafalgar Square. Cruelly, now that it was no longer possible, Hunter realised quite what he had lost, that he had wanted to marry Amy, perhaps even start a family with her. Now that would never be, and the most painful aspect of his whole sorry situation was that this was all down to him. This had all been his doing. He had been so insistent on deciphering the Lorenz code, despite being warned by two different people not to. *He* had dragged Amy to London instead of taking her to the police and safety as she had suggested, and now, thanks to him, she was gone. And where was he? No closer to the truth than before the wretched envelope had landed on his doorstep.

Hunter trudged past the front of Charing Cross Station, where rows of nervous taxi drivers prepared themselves for intemperate clientele, and street sweepers began the clean up so that London might soil itself all over again the following evening, like some giant plutocratic baby. Further off, at The Mall, someone's son or daughter was being lifted into an ambulance. The idea of being stretchered away from the world, from the hurt and the pain to somewhere warm, somewhere he might even sleep, perhaps never to re-awaken, appealed greatly to Hunter. He thought of Wiseman, that strange cantankerous old man, now dead by his own hand and perhaps finally at peace with himself. *I made a terrible mistake.* The words reverberated tunelessly around Hunter's weary head as he walked down Villiers Street towards the Embankment and the pedestrian bridge which straddled the Thames. *I made a terrible mistake.* Words which now threatened to become Hunter's very own epitaph.

He was looking for somewhere to curl up for the night, somewhere where if it rained there was a reasonable chance he might stay dry. Although he was exceptionally tired sleep seemed unthinkable. At the top of the stairs, as the bridge turned and began its long journey over dark waters, Hunter found his spot. Someone had been there before him, leaving a large square of thick, dirty cardboard. From its size and shape it might, at one time, have held a fridge or washing machine, but now it was so filthy any writing was illegible, its previous purpose a mystery. Hunter supposed its owner could return in time, but he was ready to drop and so, his precious bag clutched firmly in his arms, he slumped down and sat wearily contemplating the river as it swept beneath him, a sombre headless serpent doggedly pursuing the ocean beneath a waxing gibbous moon.

It didn't take long before Hunter's head began to drop and he succumbed to a fitful sleep. To the hundreds of people who passed him, he was just another homeless person, to be despised, pitied or ignored. He slipped deeper and deeper, into a world of disturbing and terrifying images. He dreamt only of dead people. Dead people he was unable to help, unable to save, but who cried out to him, pleaded with him, begging him to take pity on them. The strangers in Wiseman's photograph were there, their black and white mouths hanging open, wordlessly beseeching him. Joth, Wiseman, Amy. An unholy trinity now, reaching out to him, begging for his help. Then as the nightmare continued, grabbing him, pulling at his clothes, tearing them from him, whilst simultaneously pushing him away. Hunter woke with a start. He was being kicked. Not violently, just hard enough to wake him. He was confused, briefly wondering where he was. He looked up. The youth doing the kicking was about nineteen or twenty, black, powerfully built and, if his clothes were anything to go by, possibly also living rough. The owner of the cardboard?

'Is this your,' Hunter hesitated, unsure of his next word, 'bed?'

'Fuck you man! Bed! I got my own bed. What's in the bag?'

Not the owner of the cardboard but a common thief. Hunter clutched the messenger bag tightly to him, its contents all that remained of his previous life. The youth crouched down on his haunches, his large, muscular hands flat on the moist, grey paving, face thrust up close to Hunter's.

'What's in the bag, man?'

Hunter had never been in this position before, but then he thought back over the events of the previous two days. He'd been chased by an armed man, shot at and witnessed death all around him. He didn't have to stand for this. He reached into the bag. Instinctively the youth drew back. Hunter hadn't properly examined the laptop which had saved his life since the shooting, but even in the limited light of Hungerford Bridge he could see the dull brass bullet nestling amongst the bent and broken hard drive.

'There you go. Take it.' He thrust the laptop at his assailant. 'As you can see it has a bullet in it, so good luck selling that.'

'Whoa, man.'

'I've spent the day being chased and shot at. I am, as a result quite tired, so if you think you're the worst thing that's happened to me today, you are seriously fucking flattering yourself. Take it.'

Hunter sprang to his feet thrusting the ruined machine at the youth's chest.

'Come on, take it. Take it.'

'Okay man, just calm down.'

'No. The time for me to be calm is long gone my friend.' Hunter started shouting and shoving the MacBook at his attacker. 'Take it. Take it.'

'All right, I said calm down.'

'Come on you fucker. Take it!'

'Listen, I'm going okay? I'm sorry.'

'Fuck you and "sorry". What do you know about sorry? Just fuck off and leave me alone,' he shouted after the retreating figure. That had felt good. Although he'd spent the past twenty-four hours surrounded by death and destruction oddly Hunter had seldom felt more alive. He resumed his place on the cardboard and tried to get back to sleep, closing his mind to the events of the previous day, fighting to ignore the almost overpowering smell of stale urine and listening to the sound of Big Ben, born on the Thames.

***

At the far end of Hungerford Bridge, Healy and Bennett waited for the young black man to return.

'You losing your touch, Steve?'

Steve Donovan opened his hands wide and a beaming smile spread across his face.

'He really let me have it. Got quite aggro, started shoving me around and everything.'

Healy wouldn't have picked a fight with Steve Donovan unless his life had depended on it. The lad was enormous. 165 pounds of second generation, South London middle weight, and a regular at some of the gyms around Elephant and Castle.

'Sounds like someone needs to learn a few manners. Should we step in?' he suggested.

Bennett shook his head, 'Boss says not to. We'll keep an eye on him, but it sounds like he's doing fine to me. Cheers, Steve.' Bennett took a twenty pound note from his wallet.

'Any time guys, any time.'

***

It was the middle of the night when Sir John Alperton finally put the phone down. Patricia Hedley-King had called at half past ten, just as

Sir John had been packing up for the evening, about to wander down to Waterloo and catch the last train to Kent and home. She'd taken up nearly an hour and a half of his precious time all of which might have been spared if she'd said what she had to say either at their lamentable meeting in The Nightingale or by sending him a succinctly worded email. But that just wasn't her style. She was incapable of using one word when a hundred would do. Sir John had always suspected that that had in no small part contributed to her sudden and all too public fall from grace and subsequent change of career.

Now he would have to phone his wife, possibly waking her, to explain he wouldn't be coming home and then he would have to get someone to make him up the day bed in his office. He looked at the electronic cigarette Valerie had bought him. It wasn't the same, not by a long stretch but for now it would have to do, she'd made that clear. A silent edict, laid down with one slight, insinuating glance. He took a long draw on the mix of chemicals. Better. It was too late now and he didn't have the energy to skulk around the labyrinthine passages of the building simply in order to have a clandestine fag. Events were moving swifter than he would have liked or could have predicted. Once he'd spoken to his wife he'd phone Healy and Bennett and see where his boy was. When he'd last heard from them there had been some unpleasantness in Hyde Park. Shots evidently had been fired, an innocent bystander injured. This, he reflected as he took another long draw on the e-cigarette, could not be allowed to continue for very much longer, added to which he now had that frightful woman Hedley-King breathing down his neck.

Their meeting had been highly unsatisfactory from Sir John's perspective. He knew fine well what she was driving at. There had been rumours circulating The Home Office for some time. There had been other meetings with other civil servants. Other civil servants who had been a lot less guarded than Hedley-King, especially after a few glasses of thick red tongue loosener, bought by Sir John at his club, and so her dinner invitation hadn't come as a complete surprise. But Turkey? He had been shocked when she'd brought up Turkey. That had taken some balls. He jabbed the internal button on his intercom.

Bridget Crowther had been Sir John's private secretary, PA and confident for the past twenty years. Never his lover though he thought with a small twinge of regret. Bridget, it transpired, as well as being an excellent secretary was a woman of high moral principles. Sir John couldn't honestly say that he would have given her the job had he known that at the time, but now she was as trusted a member of his staff as he could imagine. And anyway, all those impulses were long forgotten, a distant memory, like so many neglected friendships.

'Yes, Sir John?'

'Bridget, could you arrange for someone to have my day bed made up for me do you think?'

'Certainly, Sir John. Will there be anything else?'

'Would you mind phoning Valerie and letting her know I'll be working late? I'm going to need a car signing out for tomorrow too.'

'I'll check and see if the BMW is available?'

'Thank you, Bridget. On second thoughts don't bother Valerie, I'll phone her myself.'

'Very good, Sir John.'

He could do with hearing a familiar voice. It would make a pleasant change to speak to a woman who was actually on *his* side. And then he'd speak to Bennett and Healy. There was never any concern about getting them out of bed.

As he waited for his wife to pick up, Alperton inspected his most recent purchase. He flicked up the tie's silken tail, inspecting the finely formed tipping and keeper. Then, out of nowhere, the most profound feeling of disappointment overcame him. Not in the tie, but in everything else, in the path he had chosen and the choices he had made, an unanswerable sense of the futility of it all, coupled with a desperate need to reach into the future and prove the old man wrong. And as quickly as it had descended on him, like a sudden and inexplicable rush of chilled air on a summer's evening, the feeling passed and his wife was sleepily answering their phone.

***

Hunter heard the coin before he saw it. It tinkled at his feet. The first of London's commuters were crossing the bridge on their way to jobs in Whitehall or The South Bank. Some kind soul had thrown Hunter a twenty pence piece causing him to smile for the first time in days. He couldn't or more accurately wouldn't get a job and had had to scrounge money from Joth and even sometimes Amy but now, when he was literally down and out, people were throwing the stuff at him.

Hunter found it almost impossible to think about Amy. His neatly ordered mind had taken the last memory of her and placed it somewhere thankfully deep and dark and necessarily unattainable and so the images left to him were frustratingly mundane; a hand on his shoulder, the daily requests that he hang up the bath mat, put away clean dishes, a badly made cup of tea from a cold pot, an argument. All the petty niggles and dissatisfactions which make up a relationship. Strange, he reasoned, that someone with such a prodigious memory should forget so readily. The worst of it, how easily he was forgetting Amy's face, her eyes.

Hunter found a discarded cup from the morning's coffee run, tore off the top edge, fanning it out to make a bigger target and placed it in front of him. He kept his head down, staring at the pavement, his hoodie pulled up and gradually over the course of the rush hour, in ones and twos, fives and tens, he'd amassed a few pounds and just enough to get him onto a tube train. He might even manage a cup of tea, if anyone would serve him. After all, it had been three days since his last shower.

During the night he hadn't slept, not really. His hands were raw and weeping and a large bruise from the shooting was forming on his back making genuine sleep almost impossible. The enforced insomnia had given him a chance to take stock. He'd gone through all the knowns and unknowns and now he had a plan. Or at least he knew how he would spend the day. Wiseman had left him two pieces of information. He'd poured over the photograph endlessly, feeling he'd taken all he could from it. That just left the manuscript. There had to be something in that manuscript connecting the photograph to his grandparents. Hunter couldn't for the life of him imagine what that might be, but he was going to spend the rest of the day reading George's memoirs in an effort to find out. Hunter needed somewhere he was unlikely to be disturbed and where he could make a quick escape if it suddenly became necessary. He'd elected to sit on the circle line and just go round and round until he'd finished. He'd always be on the move which he felt could be desirable and he'd have somewhere to sit. Thanks to the generosity of London's office workers he now had enough money for the fare and the station was just there at the bottom of the stairs.

He bought a single to Westminster, half a mile down the Embankment, allowed the rush hour to subside, hopped on a train, then went straight to the carriage at its front and was pleasantly relieved to discover only three other people, a smartly dressed city gent and a young couple, tired from travelling, their hands intertwined, her head on his shoulder. He took a seat in the corner and put the messenger bag next to him, preventing anyone sitting there, although the smell he reasoned might well have been enough.

The carriage was still littered with the morning's newspapers. He picked one up and idly flicked through it. No news of the previous day's events, even the report of the fun run in Hyde Park didn't mention any trouble and suggested the day had gone off without a hitch. There had been plenty of time before going to press. Perhaps the police had forced the media to sit on the story, but Hunter couldn't think why or if indeed the police had the powers to do such a thing. He put the paper down and took out the manuscript.

George's book had been typed on onion skin paper and then secured with treasury tags. That meant there was almost certainly a copy somewhere, probably with Wiseman's publishers. There were 264 pages, double spaced and Hunter calculated the manuscript was probably about 70 thousand words. On the title page George's farewell to him.

For Scott. I am so very sorry. I made a terrible mistake.

The delicate paper crackled with age as he turned the first page and began to read. Whilst the tube train flashed from station to station Hunter became increasingly engrossed in George's life. The opening chapter concentrated on his early days whilst working with his father at Bletchley Park and could have been lifted straight from the first book. Hunter took out his biro. Now George was dead it gave him less satisfaction, but he couldn't help himself. He underlined the word *aceptable* which seemed to be missing a C. The manuscript must have been typed at speed, George it seemed, no fan of correction fluid.

Immediately after the war George had done his stint of National Service. He'd been stationed in war torn Vienna, boxed a little for his regiment and when he wasn't doing that, acted as a liaison officer between the occupying forces, spending significant amounts of time working in the Russian quarter. He'd briefly and foolishly it seemed, fallen in love and been engaged to a local girl, but when his time in Austria had ended so had the engagement and George had returned to London and civvy street. Hunter fought the soporific swaying of the carriage and read on.

Whilst on National Service George had discovered two passions which would remain with him for the rest of his life; smoking and writing. In Vienna he'd spent every waking moment jotting down ideas and sketching out short stories and then had continued once demobbed, landing small writing jobs for some of the more respectable magazines of the time and submitting collections of short stories to interested publishers. But the real turning point in George's fortunes came in 1953 and a chance encounter with an old friend from his army days at a charity cricket match in Hampshire. Hopwood Morgan had briefly been a contemporary of George's, working with the Special Operations Executive from their headquarters at 64 Baker Street. They were both of a similar age, Wiseman hinting they had both lied about their dates of birth in order to serve King and Country. Both had had junior positions as little more than gofers, then when the war ended George joined his father at Bletchley and he and Hoppy had gone their separate ways. On Civvy Street Hopwood had exploited his experiences with The Baker Street Irregulars carving out a reputation for himself as an adviser to the spate of war films being made on both sides of the Atlantic during the early nineteen-fifties. By the time their paths crossed again Hopwood was so in demand he'd managed to get himself double booked.

Hunter rubbed a tired and twitching eye and underlined another spelling mistake.

Hoppy it seemed, had been poached from the British film he was about to start work on at Elstree Studios and was due to jet off to Hollywood and a considerably larger budget. In an effort to keep his head down and stay as far away from London and the film's understandably irate production company, Hoppy had invited himself to a friend's in Shawford, Hamps. Upon arrival he'd been quickly seconded to the local cricket team where he would later renew his friendship with George Wiseman. Would George help him out? The struggling author had been only too pleased and immediately agreed to take on the job as script editor and military adviser on a low budget film about a Dutch spy ring being run from London by the very organization he had briefly worked for during the war, the SOE.

Hunter watched another platform of exhausted Londoners as they waited for the doors to slide open and the now familiar announcements to commence.

In its own small way the film George worked on became something of a success and on the back of it he was invited to America to do a similar job for a Hollywood epic on the war in North Africa. This was all fascinating stuff and Hunter was enjoying George's tales of his early life, but he was struggling to see what on earth any of it could have to do with his grandparents. He knew his father's mother had spent a little time living and working in America, but that had been in Washington and so nearly three thousand miles away from Wiseman in Los Angeles. In any case Hunter couldn't imagine how their paths could have crossed even if they had been working in the same city as one another, as his grandmother had been an art historian, briefly employed as a curator at The National Gallery in preparation for an exhibition of the works of Mary Cassatt. Hunter was confident she had no more or less interest in films or Hollywood than anyone else. Added to which there was no reason for him to think that she and Wiseman had been in The States at the same time. Another dead end.

Hunter was about to start a new chapter in George's life when he saw them. At the far end of the train, two transport police had opened the connecting doors from the adjoining carriage and were walking purposefully towards him. All the disadvantages of such an empty compartment now abundantly clear. With a dirty thumbnail he creased the page's corner, packed away his bag, and tried to conceal his nerves. Hunter had been so engrossed in George's manuscript he hadn't noticed his hood slip down, revealing his shaven and bloodied head and to edge the hood back on now would surely attract attention. As the men drew closer Hunter picked up a discarded newspaper and pretended to be examining the back pages, the suddenness of his actions only making him feel more conspicuous. With both transport police on top of him Hunter fixed his gaze on their boots. The taller of the two men blew his nose, complaining about his hay fever, whilst his partner made for the driver's door. Hunter's hands were damp and clammy, every fibre in his body was screaming at him to run, to take flight, but to where? Whilst the first policeman exchanged pleasantries with his colleague on the other side of the secure metal door Hunter struggled to remain still and remember which station they were approaching. The acoustic inside the carriage changed subtly as the train entered the station and slowed. High Street Kensington. Hunter had as long as it took to travel the length of the platform to make his decision, although if thought about too much it did stretch credulity that anyone as scruffy and down at heal as he would be alighting at this particular platform. As he stood to move closer to the sliding doors, the sniffling policeman's partner returned and so momentarily Hunter was caught between them. Head down he mumbled an apology, edged past and hoped that they would not follow him off the train. The doors slid open and Hunter watched in the carriage window's reflection as the two policemen took up position at the centre of the train, hanging to the handrails and carrying on their conversation. Certain they would not follow, he hopped off and made his way to the escalators.

So that was where it happened. That was where Amy had been taken from him. He sat on the grass on the other side of the blue and white police flutter tape. It was still very much a crime scene, a pair of bored looking WPCs stood next to the Peter Pan Monument trying to keep out of the sun. Hunter was growing used to the new found anonymity his look afforded him even if his head did still smart where he had repeatedly nicked it. There in the distance were the Italian Gardens. The chase seemed as though it had happened a lifetime ago. But Amy's death, her murder, burnt hot in his memory. The instant that she had been shot would live with him forever, a little like one of Wiseman's bloody photographs. He took out the manuscript and located the page with its bent corner.

The next couple of chapters concentrated on George's move to LA and his newfound lifestyle. He mixed with Hollywood's great and good, on one occasion finding himself sat next to Orsen Wells at dinner. It wasn't difficult for Hunter to imagine how the Americans would have lapped up George's debonair dress sense, cut glass accent and impeccable manners. There was a man who, if he chose to, could charm the very birds from the trees. But he was interested to see that Wiseman wasn't just mixing with Hollywood's creative types, he had also been introduced to some of America's foremost politicians. He'd met Senator Pat McCarran, author of the infamous 1950 anti-communist act that bore his name. He'd been introduced to Adlai Stevenson who had gone on to run unsuccessfully against Eisenhower in the 1956 Presidential Election and he was a regular dinner guest of Alan Greenspan the global economist and recently appointed chairman of the Federal Reserve. Whatever George had been up to he was doing it at a pretty high level. *Posession* Hunter noted seemed to be missing an S. He underlined it.

Hunter flicked back. Just a few pages before he had seen *coresppondence* and underlined that too. He hadn't to turn too many pages over before he found another and then another. In the first fifty pages he found ten spelling mistakes, each spaced five pages from the previous one. And not just errors where the wrong letters had been used. No. Each time there was an actual letter missing. He turned over the next five pages and started reading. George was treading the red carpet at a black tie launch, George was drinking daiquiris and horsing around with Cary Grant and a surprisingly ribald David Niven, George was struggling with a tactfully anonymous writer's poorly written script. And there it was, *originaly* missing its L. This was happening far too regularly to be a coincidence. Hunter went back to the beginning and every five pages, when he found a mistake, he wrote the letter at the top of the corresponding page. Quickly he had a sequence of eleven letters. They didn't spell anything but Hunter recognised them instantly. What had Wiseman said? In one respect they all look the same. That clever old bastard. He'd hidden a code in his unpublished memoirs. He'd said Hunter was the only one who would understand it and now he did. Yes, Hunter thought, you did make a terrible mistake and if I'm correct you've made about forty more.

Hunter was so engrossed he'd forgotten about the two police women. They were walking towards him. Best be off. In any case, if he were to decode Wiseman's message he was going to need a new laptop and his programme back from Alec.

He retraced his steps to High Street Ken. and found a little café. It was packed, ideal for Hunter to lose himself in. But he must be careful. The men inside were probably construction workers or taxi drivers, judging by their attire, but it was also just the sort of place the police might stop by for a quick cuppa. He scanned the interior then walked past twice, snatching furtive glances before moving quickly on. Satisfied he could lose himself and that there was an empty table towards the rear next to a fire escape, he went in. There was a friendly buzz about the place and no one paid him any attention. He'd guessed right and now he was inside he could see the black cab driver's leather IDs almost everywhere. The only table not full of boisterous tea swilling taxi drivers entertaining four labourers in grubby T-shirts and high-viz waist coats, their hard hats competing for space with yawning plates of English breakfast. The quartet were animatedly discussing the previous night's football results as Hunter passed, gazing longingly at their food. He took a seat at the last table with the fire exit to his side. There was just enough for a sweet cup of tea plus 20 pence to call Alec. He'd see how long he could make the tea last before the woman running the place threw him out. With the manuscript in front of him he picked up from where he'd left off, skipping ahead to where he suspected George had inserted a mistake. Every so often he checked one of the other pages finding them all perfectly spelt, but every fifth page, as he'd expected there would be, there was a freshly misspelled word. George, at another opening night party. George, having dinner with a minor American politician. George, working on the set of a new Hollywood war film. Hunter's list of letters was growing steadily longer.

'You running away from home, dear?'

The owner stood over him. He would have to find somewhere else.

'Yes, yes I suppose I am.'

She was a kindly looking woman, probably late forties, early fifties with a mop of unruly blond hair, shockingly overweight and smelling of stale tobacco she wheezed at the slightest exertion. Unbidden she poured Hunter a fresh cup of tea.

'Thank you.' This simple act of maternalistic kindness following the previous few days was almost enough to break him.

'You got a family, dear?' Hunter pushed his saucer around nervously. 'Well, you must be somebody's son, eh?'

'Yes.'

'Call 'em. Just to let 'em know you're okay,' she said then shuffled off back behind her counter. Hunter had the distinct impression there was some dreadful personal experience wrapped up in her last remark. He took the phone from his bag. Dead.

On the back of the last page of George's manuscript Hunter compiled the fifty-two spelling mistakes. Through force of habit he put them in capital letters and in groups of four. Once he'd finished there was no longer any doubt in his mind, he was looking at a code and he desperately needed his laptop. The tea gone and the owner of the café thanked and reassured he headed off to find a phone box and a computer shop.

Phone boxes, or at least phone boxes which worked, were pretty thin on the ground in this part of London. The only place Hunter thought he might find one was the tube station. He waited for the beeping to stop and inserted the twenty pence piece. Alec's answer phone. He swore as he listened to his friend's voice and then left a quick message.

On the other side of High Street Ken. station there was a huge electrical store which seemed to sell every product under the one roof, everything from fridges and freezers to mobile phones and televisions. Most importantly they sold laptops. Hunter knew he would never get away with lifting something from the shop, all the machines were secured with vinyl-coated, tamper-resistance cable, making them almost impossible to steal, but if he could get on line with one of the store's demonstration models he might get at his software and feed the code straight in. Hunter had been in this type of shop hundreds of times before. He'd spent much of his student life in electronics stores, buying upgrades or drooling over the most recent releases. He knew what to expect, tables laid out with the latest kit. They'd all be on so that customers could come and play and the store was sure to have a secure wi-fi connection so that the staff could demonstrate any internet capability. It would be password protected but Hunter had a good record of working out passwords created by lazy shop assistants. They had to be something that every member of staff could easily recall and in Hunter's experience ranged from PASSWORD to the name of the store. If they were feeling particularly creative they sometimes included a number. Given enough time he would have his programme up and running in the background and no one would be any the wiser. Then it would simply be a case of staying out of the way of the police and returning before the store shut to see what the algorithm had turned up. Additionally, if he was lucky he might get a chance to charge his mobile phone, although he wasn't sure he was ready for the messages he expected to find.

Hunter threw back his shoulders and brushed off some of the filth which had accrued over the previous few days. He'd had to acknowledge there was nothing to be done about the smell, but for now he would try his best to appear like a respectable member of society. Shoppers were busily coming and going and if he timed his entrance well he might tag on the end of a group and enter the store unnoticed by the security guard. A mother and father were cajoling two reluctant teenage daughters. Hunter fell in line behind the taller of the pair as their parents activated the first pair of glass doors. The shop's security guard continued to pace absently in the coconut-matted no man's land between the outside world and admittance. The parents entered the shop, the father taking off with renewed purpose, but just as Hunter was about to pass through the first set of sliding doors, one of the girls stopped abruptly in her tracks and, brandishing her mobile phone, embarked on an argument with her sister. Hunter almost walked straight into the back of the girl. Feeling awkwardly conspicuous he decided to make his move past the bickering family. As he stepped out from the shadows, and nearly at the second set of doors, the guard, drawn by the sound of raised voices turned and with two calculated strides, blocked his path. He took one long, lingering look at Hunter, shook his head and wordlessly resumed his station by the sliding doors, like a bouncer at a night club. Hunter got the message. He wasn't stupid. In fact, if the boot had been on the other foot he would probably have done the same. He sidled out past the feuding sisters and was just deciding what to do next when a huge bank of television screens which had previously been entertaining passers-by with football highlights switched over to Sky News.

Police still hunting killer of Cambridge students

There were photographs of Joth and Amy taken from the university's records and then, whilst Hunter was trying to recover from the shock of seeing them again and the confirmation of their deaths, a fresh face filled the screen. This photograph had not come from the university. It was much glossier. A professional headshot, taken by a professional photographer, for a professional member of the media. Hunter looked through his glassy reflection at Alec Bell's fresh, smiling face. He'd been shot in the university grounds and the police weren't hesitating in connecting the three murders. Lastly, after some shaky mobile phone footage of proud runners showing off their medals, Hunter watched himself running frantically in the background and then the chaotic scenes from Hyde Park. There was an interview with the runner he had vaulted over. The man was lying in a hospital bed, his leg heavily bandaged and raised, his teary wife by his side. Hunter didn't need to see any more. He knew what was coming next. He pulled the hoodie close over his head, turned and walked away.

There was nothing for it. There was only one place left to turn. The money had gone, what little of it there had been and he wasn't prepared to spend another evening begging on the streets of London. He was tired, hungry and he had the feeling that it was not going to be a dry night for the capital. Storm clouds were gathering. If he could make it as far as the shopping centre at Brent Cross he'd try to thumb a lift up the M1 from there. He had a vague idea that if he could get to the Edgware Road that would lead him up through Kilburn and eventually to the bottom of the motorway. He didn't know how far it was, five miles maybe six? If he pressed on he should be there by early evening. The walk might give him a chance to think, although he already had a good idea what the new code would prove to be.

***

Wet and exhausted Hunter arrived at Brent Cross just as many of the shops were shutting. At Cricklewood it had started to rain and so by the time he'd navigated the North Circular, Hunter was soaked through. Near Dollis Hill he'd walked passed one electrical store after another without even bothering to gain admittance, the walk giving him precious time to think on George's enigmatic final message and how his grandfather might possibly be involved. The car parks of Brent Cross were beginning to empty and with the prospect of another miserable night out in the cold looming, Hunter disappeared behind one of the superstores to the loading bays at their rear and found an old piece of discarded cardboard.

Beaten and defeated, he stood at the exit to the car park, surrounded by the detritus of modern travel, a rudimentary sign in his bandaged hand. There were single sodden and muddy shoes, often children's, washed up next to drainage covers, fast food packaging and used condoms. All things that made Hunter wonder about their previous owners. He'd simply written *NORTH* over and over itself, in fine, spindly biro. He would jump out of the car whenever it was convenient or the questions became too awkward. One or two drivers had slowed down and he'd thought he might be in luck, but the first had been a woman making a phone call and the second a car full of young lads who'd wound the windows down and screamed abuse at him. Another cold night under the stars was beginning to look increasingly likely.

Then, as cars continued to leave, he saw the black BMW 6 series. It was the same car Hunter had seen parked on Danforth Road, the same car he had glimpsed as he ran from McAllister's on the Tottenham Court Road and the same car he'd walked past on Lansdowne Terrace. With nothing to lose, he strode up to the driver's side and rapped on the window. The tinted glass disappeared effortlessly revealing a man in his mid-sixties, impeccably dressed but clearly not to be trifled with. One look at his suit told Hunter it was hand tailored, possibly from the Savile Row, probably from somewhere a little more exclusive just off the Savile Row. His shirt was freshly ironed and pressed, his tie pure silk and probably worth more than all of Hunter's clothes combined. A peculiar smell issued from the car's cosseted interior, a strange mixture of tobacco and vanilla. Hunter struggled to identify it before spotting the thick e-cigarette lying near the dashboard.

'Get in,' the man said tersely before Hunter could open his mouth.

'Get in,' he repeated. 'I'm a friend. I can take you as far as Chandler's Cross, but after that you're on your own.'

The man certainly seemed to know exactly where Hunter was headed. Chandler's Cross would leave him a walk of a couple of miles. If he knew where he was intending to go then he knew who he was and who he intended to see. He also probably knew a great deal more. Hunter was too tired, too wet and too hungry to argue. Without a word he climbed into the passenger seat.

The BMW was a smooth ride and his driver had the heating set up just a little higher than was necessary on a spring evening. They hardly made it to the M1 before Hunter's eyes started to close and by junction 2 he was fast asleep.

10

The elegantly dressed gentleman was as good as his word. Hunter woke as they slowed to turn off the M25 and dozed the remainder of the way to the sleepy little hamlet of Chandlers Cross. The car stopped at a fork in the road.

'This is where we part company, Scott.'

Something in the way the man spoke stopped Hunter from asking how he knew his name. Reticently he thought of George Wiseman and wondered if he could grab the man's expensive silk tie, jam it through the steering wheel and force some answers from him, but the smartly dressed gent was uncompromisingly built. Hunter had had an English teacher with a similar physique and air. One lunchtime he'd watched him lift a sixth former clean off his feet and throw him from the school quads. He didn't doubt for one moment that the man sat coolly to his right was every bit as capable, gentlemen are not always gentle-men, after all.

'Thank you,' Hunter mumbled before opening the door. As he leant back to retrieve his bag the man lit a cigarette.

'Good luck, Scott,' he said, 'I hope you find what you're looking for.' He never turned to face Hunter, brooding into the night, the cigarette never far from his lips.

The Sarratt Road was little more than a country lane. There was no artificial light and the tall hedgerows made it feel darker still. Briefly the lane opened out and Hunter found himself walking over the motorway he had just left. None of this was new to him, these were well-worn paths, desire lines both real and imagined, and the closer he came to his destination the more familiar and well-worn they felt. Familiar, yet not comfortable. Leaving the M25 roaring behind him Hunter arrived on the outskirts of the village. There were two tartly isolated houses and then, finally the sign welcoming him to Sarratt and inviting him to drive carefully. Now the butterflies were beginning to mount. As he pressed on into the more residential heart of the village here and there the signs of everyday life. Radios and television sets turned up high to drown out empty lives. Couples exchanging workaday banalities, guarded precursors to love or war and cruelly, rising above the hubbub, the smell of home cooking, of shop bought curries and pizzas competing with sweated onions and garlic. Half a mile further on he saw the green. The pubs were still open but Hunter couldn't imagine for how much longer.

He walked past The Boot with its gnarled old trees and turned off and up the lane which ran down its side. He was close now. Horses were still out in their paddocks, loudly snorting the night air. He stopped. Was he really going to do this, was he really going to seek refuge from the one man whose deceit had caused him so much pain? His shoes crackled over the gravel as he walked up the driveway to his father's house.

David Hunter spent most of the evening in his garden. He slipped on a blue knitted cardigan, poured himself a glass of chilled

Gewürztraminer and idly strolled around in his slippers inspecting the various shrubs. He dead headed some of the early bloomers then tried unenthusiastically to tie back a brutish clematis but with little success. Then he sat on the bench at the back of the house and listened to the blackbirds, keeping his glass topped up from the cooler by his side and enjoying the warm damp air. He'd been delighted with his work on the Anniversary clock, but much of his pleasure had been soured when the previous day had brought with it unwanted visitors bearing sad and disturbing news.

David finished locking up for the night. He knew many of his neighbours didn't bother but he was a Londoner at heart and liked the reassurance of latched windows and bolted doors. When he had moved out to the country he'd scoured the area for just the right property, somewhere that would afford him the level of privacy he desired. There had been a cottage in Tring, about fifteen miles away, which he'd been very taken with, but had quickly come to realise was a sum of its parts. Take away the owners' furniture, curtains and beautiful artworks and it was nothing.

He was rinsing a glass at the sink when he heard the first tentative knock. It was late and he was not expecting anyone. Living where he did it was most unusual to receive guests, that had been one of the reasons for moving there. He put down the wine glass and walked through into the dining room, ducking as he passed under the cottage's low dark beams to where the finished clock sat. It seemed to be working perfectly now, under its new protective glass dome. Another knock, stronger this time, even a little insistent. It could be Jerry from up the lane. His horses did get out from time to time and

David had, on one occasion, somewhat reluctantly offered him a hand. He squinted down the fisheye lens. No, not Jerry. A scruffy young man. Probably some poor sod, down on his luck, selling shammy leathers and gimmicks for the garden. David would be polite but firm and get rid of him.

He stared at the figure on his doorstep. His clothes were filthy and damp and it was hard for David to make out his face as he wore a hood pulled tight over his head. He looked pale and thin with the beginnings of a beard framing hollow sunken eyes. In his hand a bag of sorts, like its owner, tired and dirty and David presumed, full of the wares he intended to hawk. And then the visitor pulled back his hood revealing his closely shaven head, lines and scars criss-crossing his scalp amidst the smears of dried blood.

'Scott?' David looked at his son. He'd been so desperate to see him, but he'd never wanted to see him like this.

'Hello.'

'Oh my God, Scott, come in. Let me take that,' David said gesturing to his son's bag, but Hunter kept it held close to him. 'I've had the police looking for you. They said,' David could hardly bring himself to say it, 'they said that... that Amy's dead.'

Scott nodded silently, hardly noticing as his father led him into the sitting room.

'Scott, are you all right? Dear God, what happened?'

'I watched her die. I watched her die right in front of me and there was nothing I could do to save her.'

'They said she'd been shot?'

Hunter nodded.

'Oh Scott. I'm so very sorry. You know I really thought...'

'I know.'

The silent years of unanswered telephone calls descended between them. Hunter knew what his father was thinking all too well.

'It was my fault. It's my fault she's dead.' Hunter's large emotionless eyes stared blankly back at his father. There were no tears left, only silence.

'You look shocking. Can I get you something? Something to eat, a cup of tea?'

'Have you got anything stronger? Whisky?'

'I'll see what I can do.'

David disappeared into the kitchen and Hunter listened as long-abandoned cupboards were plundered and glasses and a bottle found. As he waited for his father, and with the house's warmth slowly penetrating his body and his strength starting to return Hunter carefully took in his surroundings. Everything was much as he could remember. There had been subtle changes here and there, some of the paintings on the walls had been re-arranged, there were fresh biographies on the bookshelves and a new and expensive looking piece of hi-fi blinked lazily in its cabinet, but by and large much the same. The same overbearing oak furniture, the dresser badly scratched, the same clapped out computer, the same dining table his father had invested so much time in. And that was when he saw the clock. This was new. He crossed the room to examine it more closely. David joined him and they stood silently contemplating the magnificent domed timepiece and their drinks.

'Sorry, I don't know how you take it.'

'That's all right. Neither do I.' He knocked back a measure. 'Nice clock.'

'Thank you. I've just finished a little restoration work.'

Hunter nodded at his father's craftsmanship.

'Difficult job?'

'Harder than you might imagine, yes. It belonged to your mother, you know?'

'I see.' Hunter drained the last of his whisky and put the glass on the table next to the clock. How dare he mention his mother. How dare he bring her up at a time like this. The man was a liar and a cheat. Why couldn't he just have lied about the clock too?

'All I need from you is your computer. Then I'll go.'

'I understand.' David took the glass from the table. 'Although I'm not convinced that you do, Scott.'

'What the hell do you mean by that? I know you don't want me here in your cosy little palace.'

David was going to ignore the comment but then changed his mind.

'Why *are* you here exactly, Scott?'

'I had nowhere else to go, I can assure you of that.'

David was inclined to believe him. He could see the effort involved in his son's visit and the resentment too.

'You still haven't told me *why* Amy was killed? People aren't simply shot in the middle of Hyde Park for no reason. The police told me about Joth and Alec. Three people dead, Scott. You need to tell me what's been going on.'

'Four dead, actually. Old guy. Sick, probably dying, not that that matters now. Claimed to have all the answers. Killed himself.' David flinched at mention of the suicide.

'You'd better tell me everything. But first I think I'm going to need another drink.'

Whilst his father filled their glasses Hunter emptied the contents of his bag onto the dining room table; the black and white photograph, George's manuscript and the copy of his first book.

'How long have you been drinking neat whisky?' David asked offering him a glass.

'Since I met this guy.' Hunter turned the copy of Wiseman's book over to show his father the publicity shot on the back. 'Now he's dead, probably no thanks to me.'

'I see,' his father said looking away.

'He took care of us, me and Amy.'

'Yes, I know.'

'You know? What do you mean you know?'

'He called me.'

'Wiseman called *you*?'

'Yes.'

'Why the hell would Wiseman call you?'

'To tell me you were safe.'

'He never mentioned he knew you. How do you know him?'

'Like I said, there's still a lot you don't understand. He was a good man, Scott.'

'He said he had information. Something about Papa.'

'Ah. No, it wasn't your Papa,' David said shaking his head, 'Your grandfather. Did you say you needed a computer?'

'Yes. I'm going to need a sharp knife too.'

'I'll get you one. I think it's about time you see something you should probably have seen years ago, Scott. You know where the PC is? Help yourself.'

Whilst Hunter waited for his father's elderly computer to boot up he removed one of the USB cables from the printer. Taking the Sabatier his father had fetched from the kitchen he pried off the printer pin and began exposing its wires. With the tip of the knife he undid two screws at the base of his phone. Hunter teased out the battery, inserted the bare cable where the electric contacts came in and then replaced the battery. His father's computer was finally on and he plugged in the USB to a free port. A quick waggle of the cables and the phone began to charge. Then he went online and directly to his dropbox account. Thank God, Alec had left the algorithm in place and not dragged it to his desktop. He ran the programme and began the laborious task of inputting the second code Wiseman had left him hidden in his manuscript. His phone gave a bleep and started to reboot.

***

With his free hand David found the light switch. He'd brought a torch this time and went straight for the second and smaller cardboard box. Without thinking he shone the torch inside but then hesitated, suddenly anxious he was doing the right thing. A long beat, then David Hunter nodded to himself, picked up the box, turned off the light and folded away the ladders.

Hunter was bent over his father's computer when his phone burst into life. There were texts from his service provider instructing him to pick up messages and more from concerned friends enquiring after his whereabouts and wellbeing. He dialled 121 and started retrieving and discarding the twelve messages which had built up over the previous few days. There were several from both the Cambridge and Metropolitan police requiring him to get in touch urgently and leaving numbers for him to ring and then a voice that made his blood run cold. There was a message from Alec.

'Hello mate, thanks for the email. I ran your programme and got a bunch of names. Nothing to write home about, although I did recognise one of them. Dietrich Metzger. I read about him a couple of years ago for a paper I was writing. Big-time German physicist before the war. Studied at Heidelberg but then just disappeared. I thought about trying to find out what happened to him but well… that's more your kind of thing? Anyway, hope you're okay. Love to Ames.'

Hunter put down the iPhone, still connected and charging, and stared at it. So, Metzger had been a physicist and one with enough of a reputation to catch Alec's eye. His father appeared with a grubby looking old shoe box and laid it down on the table next to the clock. The PC sprang to life and code started pouring down the screen. Hunter tapped a few keys and a second list began to appear.

J Whitehead
D Butcher

P Drake

H Honeycutt

Four names and then the programme crashed, frozen, too much for his father's antiquated machine to deal with. Hunter pointed to the screen. He'd been right, there had been a second list, but who were these people? He found the photograph taken from Wiseman's flat and flicked it over. The initials of the Christian names were the same. He went into the guts of the programme, located the problem and re-ran it, leaving his father to look through the dusty old box.

J Whitehead

D Butcher

P Drake

H Honeycutt

The next name on the back of Wiseman's photograph was J A Seidel. Hunter prayed his father's computer would co-operate just a little while longer and then, to his relief, a fifth name was added to the list before the programme stalled again.

J Sinclair.

Sinclair. What the hell was Sinclair's name doing there? Admittedly this was J Sinclair but then hadn't Wiseman mentioned a Josef Sinclair? Coincidence? Scott looked at his father but was only struck by how unsurprised he appeared.

'There's one last name, but I can't get the bloody programme to work and your computer isn't exactly helping much either.'

'There's no need,' his father said, 'I can tell you the last name on your list.'

Hunter realised that whilst they had been talking his father had been holding a small black and white photograph. David placed it on the computer desk in front of his son. It was the same photograph Hunter had first seen cropped in Wiseman's book at the library in Trinity College. It was the same photograph he had taken from the dead man's apartment. A photograph of George Wiseman and his father sat rather smartly behind a table and a Second World War Lorenz machine, behind them, in a line, five men and one woman. It was the same photograph Hunter still held in his hand and was convinced contained all the answers. So, what the hell was his father doing with a copy?

'He,' David said pointing to a stern looking young man in his late twenties, 'was Friedrich Ritthaler. In 1948, with some help from George Wiseman and his father, he became Frank Richards. Your mother's father. Your grandfather.'

Hunter didn't understand. This was a picture of, well who was it a picture of exactly? He'd never properly known had he, that had been the problem. Suddenly he realised just how little he knew about the maternal side of his family.

David was pointing at the other members of the line.

'There's Metzger and that's Seidel. The woman was called Schmid, she became Honeycutt. These two men are Utkin and Borkowski although I'm afraid I can't recall which one is which now.'

'How do you know all this? Who were they and why did they have their names changed?'

'One thing at a time, Scott. It was chaos at the end of the Second World War. America had just demonstrated the bomb and only ten years later the Russians started the space race and in the intervening time the East and West plunged headlong into the Cold War.'

'Metzger was a physicist.'

'Of a sort, yes. After the war there was a huge sweep up. The allies called it Operation Paperclip. Wernher von Braun went to The States to help start NASA and their race for the moon, Doctors Hoch and Blazig went the other way to Russia and their space programme, along with tonnes of salvaged rocket parts from Peenemünde. But there were many more. Many who, for one reason or another, simply disappeared, either of their own volition or because the governments of the countries they were helping thought it expedient.'

'What did he do?' Hunter asked pointing at the man in the photograph. His father thought for a moment.

'He was a chemist. I didn't really understand a great deal about the work he was involved in, but I was lead to believe that he possessed an...' again David struggled to find the correct word, 'an unusual talent.'

'And what was Wiseman's role in all of this?'

'When they arrived, mostly from Germany, but Utkin and Borkowski both came from Russia via Vienna, there was an initial quite lengthy period of incarceration and questioning. We had to be absolutely certain these people were who they said they were. By the time that photograph was taken Wiseman and his father had created

211

whole new identities for them. You see it wasn't just important for them to blend into British society. We were always on the guard against the Americans and the Russians. They would have spirited them away at the drop of a hat had they found out who they were.'

David went back to the shoe box and took out an oily mass, wrapped in a large black rag. He found some newspaper and covered a portion of the table. Whatever was in the rag was heavy and metallic. He carefully removed it and to Hunter's horror placed it on the newspaper in front of him. A Super-Star semi-automatic pistol.

'These were given to all of the people in that photograph, including your grandfather.' David picked it up, pressed the magazine release button, removed and checked it, then swiftly pushed the magazine firmly back into the pistol and locked the catch. He quickly checked the safety and placed it back on the table. 'It's never been fired.' David rubbed his oily hands on his trousers. Hunter had never seen his father handle a gun before. He looked closely at the man standing next to him, the man who had brought him up. Where had a lowly accounts exec. who'd taken early retirement and a considerable golden handshake learnt how to strip a gun? Hunter realised for the first time how little he knew about the man who was his father.

'Is this the only picture you have of him?'

'No, your mother left papers for you.'

'I don't understand. Why have I never seen any of them before?' But David was leaving the room. Hunter turned to the table and the oily black gun that lay there. Tentatively he picked it up, weighing it in his hand. It felt cold and foreign. There was the safety catch, it was on he assumed. He rubbed the excess oil from its grip onto his already filthy clothes and quickly slipped it into the front pocket of his hoodie. He could hear his father returning.

David had an envelope containing no more than a dozen photographs. Hunter noted that in each of the pictures his grandfather stood alone. There were no wedding photographs, no pictures of him with Hunter's mother, yet in each picture there was that same stern expression. There was something unrepentant in the man's eyes, something challenging and confrontational. Something which Hunter found deeply disturbing. He couldn't deny his grandfather had been a handsome man, tall but not thin, his hair pushed back and brylcreamed in place in the style of the time. But there was something else. An arrogance. It gave him no pleasure to think that he was related to the man who stared so aggressively back at him. Added to which, Scott couldn't help but notice just how little interest his father expressed in any of the photographs.

'How well did you know him?'

'Well enough,' David said with expedience.

'And where are the pictures of his family? His wife? Mum?'

'Listen Scott, when your mother died a lot of things got thrown away. This is all that's left. I'm sorry.'

Hunter took a sip from his glass. So, the lists were a relocation programme for Second World War scientists. That went some way to explain the secrecy and George's reluctance to speak of them. His own grandfather had been a chemist called Ritthaler who the Wisemans had spirited out of Germany in 1945. He'd been given a new identity and a gun. After the war and now called Frank Richards he'd met Hunter's grandmother and started a family. However none of this explained why a six foot something ape covered in tattoos and sporting a menacing biker's ring had killed three people and chased Hunter halfway across London in an effort to kill him too. Nor did it shed any light on his new found friend who besides having expensive tastes in both clothes and cars, was clearly, and somewhat unsuccessfully, trying to quit smoking. Scott held up his glass for a top up and to get his father out of the way.

'We need to talk.'

The voice on the other end of the line agreed, suggesting a meeting place.

Hunter knew it and could be there in an hour and a half. 'Yes, I know what time it is, but I've seen the second list.' Without waiting for a reaction he replaced the receiver, his iPhone still charging. In the bottom of his bag he found a mobile number casually scrawled on a scrappy piece of paper. He flicked his iPhone on, opened the contacts list and entered the details before sending a brief text message. His father had returned with a large scotch and some bread and butter which Hunter devoured greedily, pushing the drink to one side. Then he was up and out of his seat, throwing everything into the messenger bag, everything except Wiseman's manuscript.

'What are we going to do with this?'

Whilst his father considered, Hunter moved across the room and stood next to the small open fireplace at its heart. He looked at his father, implicitly seeking permission.

'Do it.'

On top of the mantlepiece, amongst the candles and tea lights, a small box of matches. Hunter tore out Wiseman's cryptic apology and page after page followed as he and his father watched them smoulder and burn until the hearth danced with flames.

'Will I make up the spare bed?'

'I'm not staying.'

'Scott, let's talk about this.'

'It's not that.'

'You're exhausted, you need to sleep. We can pick this up in the morning, go and see the police.'

'No.'

'Try and explain you've done nothing wrong.' David was terrified he was about to lose his son for a second time.

'There's someone I have to see first.'

David Hunter looked down and away, all his fears realised in that one sentence, the years of deceit all for nothing.

'Are they where they usually are?' Hunter was by the front door, going through his father's jacket pockets. 'No police. I'm not ready to explain anything yet. Something's still not right.' He held up the keys to his father's aged Volvo.

'What are you doing?'

'Steeling your car, father,' Hunter said opening the door. 'Don't forget, I'm a fugitive wanted by the police.'

David was quickly behind him. 'Scott. *Scott!*' His son turned to face him. 'The car's one thing but that,' he said, pointing to the heavy bulge in his son's top, 'is quite another. No father should see his son going off god knows where with a loaded gun.' He held out his hand as only a father can to his son.

Reluctantly Scott took the pistol from his hoodie and laid it in David Hunter's open palm.

David flicked the safety off, racked the slide allowing it to spring forward into the closed position and flicked the safety back.

'There's a round in the chamber and the safety's on. So, where are we going?' he asked slipping on a pair of comfortable shoes.

'Cambridge.'

11

They drove in an uneasy silence, as is often the way with fathers and their sons, Hunter sitting grimly behind the wheel, struggling to come to terms with what he had just learnt. Whilst he was closer to understanding the two lists, now something else preoccupied him, something, or rather someone, significantly closer to home. The man sitting to his left, the man who, through the years he had blamed for so much. There was clearly another side to his father. A side which, like the clock, he had taken great care to hide from his son. Why had George Wiseman called him in the middle of the night and how did his father know the erstwhile author-cum-spy, and where had he learnt to handle a gun like that? How many more broken clocks were there, how many more secret-laden dusty old cardboard boxes sat rotting in David Hunter's attic? With every passing minute, as the awkward silence settled and established itself, the questions which burnt so fiercely inside Scott Hunter, only became more difficult to ask.

David by contrast was feeling quietly content. He'd wanted to unburden himself for so long and yet even now, as the end drew near, he knew the story was far from told. His son would certainly have many more questions, but at least the impasse had been broken and they had arrived at an uneasy truce. David Hunter felt that for the first time in years they were bonding, he allowed himself to dream a little, like a family. He was no fool though. When Scott knew everything, when he saw the whole dark horrible truth, well then they'd see.

The motorway was clear. Hunter passed the occasional lorry but his father's Volvo wasn't capable of any great turn of speed and so he contented himself with the slow lane. The man he was going to meet would wait for him, he was confident of that if nothing else. The dull glint of gun metal caught his eye. His father had put the semi-automatic on the floor next to his feet where it skittered around in the footwell. What the hell were they doing? Hunter wasn't sure, but he was certain that he wouldn't go into another confrontation without some way of defending himself.

✳✳✳

David followed his son into the boathouse which perched so easily on the banks of the Cam, the handle of the Super-Star pistol poking out of the top of his trousers, concealed by his undulating cardigan.

Hunter took it all in. He'd been here many times before with Alec. Hanging from their cradles the carbon-fibre eights, along the walls ranks of sweep oars and delicate individual sculls. Two rowing boats neatly stowed away in one corner. Triumphant caps and pendants displayed exultantly from every spare inch of wall. And then, from the shadows stepped Professor Frederick Sinclair, his normally impeccable hair a touch out of place due to the hour, his quasi sailing shoes suddenly starkly inappropriate in the surroundings.

'Scott. I'm so pleased to see you. Whatever have you been up to? I've had the police asking all sorts of questions,' he began awkwardly, fiddling with his poorly knotted tie. And then seeing Scott was not alone, 'and who's this you've brought with you?'

'My father.'

Sinclair stepped closer, peering over his spectacles to examine David in the gloom of the boathouse before extending a cordial hand.

'How very pleasant to meet you,' he said, 'although I feel I know so very much about you already,' he added with a sickly smile.

'Do you?'

Sinclair withdrew his hand but not his gaze.

'Scott, am I to take it you have had more success with that computer programme of yours?'

Hunter nodded.

'I've seen both lists if that's what you mean?'

Sinclair inclined his head, musing quietly to himself.

'You left me that code. Why?' Hunter asked.

Sinclair seemed surprised by the intrusion into his private thoughts.

'No. No I did not actually. I genuinely have no idea as to the origins of that message, although I do have my suspicions,' he continued raising an eyebrow in David Hunter's direction. 'No, like you I should very much like to know exactly where that has been hiding all these years. And you came by the second list how?'

'George Wiseman.'

'George. Of course, I should have known he'd have kept a copy. How is the interfering old fool?'

'Dead.' Again Sinclair nodded his understanding. 'Suicide,' Hunter added, causing his professor to smile.

'Ah, what a grand gesture, how terribly theatrical of old George,' Sinclair said never once taking his eyes from David's. 'He always was one for a spot of melodrama. I put it down to all those years mucking about with poofs and pinkoes. And you have the lists with you I take it, otherwise there would be no need for this clandestine little tête-à-tête?' Sinclair extended his hand ready to receive the information.

'I know everything,' said Hunter as confidently as he was able.

'Oh, I doubt that,' Sinclair laughed, 'I doubt that very much, Scott. If you knew everything, I doubt you would be here at all. Isn't that right, David?' The use of his father's Christian name shocked Hunter. More secrets. 'The lists please?'

Hunter opened his arms. 'I don't have them.'

'Really? That is a shame.'

Sinclair retreated into the shadows allowing the hulking figure Hunter had last seen pursuing him through the fountains of Hyde Park to emerge, in one hand the silenced pistol. The giant's other hand Hunter noted with a small degree of satisfaction was heavily bandaged, the silver ring still evident.

'So, now we're all here I'm going to ask you again. Where are the lists?'

David stepped forward, positioning himself between Hunter and the professor. 'I burnt them. What good can they do now? Isn't it time we put all this behind us? There's been enough death, hasn't there?'

'Oh, David. Ever the voice of reason, weren't you? Always trying to do the right thing, as I recall. And always failing.'

Sinclair brushed past David and the giant followed. 'He still has them.' The professor stood directly in front of Hunter. 'They're up here,' he said pointing at Hunter's temple, 'and that, I cannot have.'

'Leave him,' David pleaded, but the giant stood over his son, gun in hand barring his path.

'That memory of yours, Scott. It should have lead to such great things, but you just wouldn't apply yourself, would you? You squandered your God given talents. Are you simply lazy? No, I'm not sure that's quite right. Was it Alec? Poor Alec, he always got everything you desired, didn't he Scott?'

'No! You don't talk about her. You don't even say her name.' Hunter lunged at Sinclair but found his progress barred by a thick tattooed arm, 'You filthy bastard.'

'I can see how that must have hurt you. Every time you saw him, did you think about her? Did you imagine the pair of them lying together, in his bed?'

'I understand now.' Hunter had wanted to control his emotions, but Sinclair was goading him, 'I understand why she found you so repulsive. She was everything you could never be,' he shouted over the indelible black swirls, 'She possessed everything you could never have.'

'She was a butterfly, Scott, moving from man to man.'

Again Hunter tried to reach Sinclair, to hurt him and again he was beaten away, the giant loosing a vicious backhand, the ring catching Hunter crisply above his eye. He felt the skin split and gape, the blood trickle down the side of his face.

'She was tolerant, compassionate and loving. Things you'll never understand.'

'How wonderfully sentimental you are, Scott. Really I had no idea. Although I have to agree, she certainly seemed "loving".'

'You're a murderer and a coward.'

Sinclair considered the statement before stepping behind Hunter and speaking softly in his ear.

'Let us talk about cowardice, shall we? Maybe,' he said choosing each word with infinite care, 'maybe if your mother hadn't killed herself in quite such an act of puritanical self-pity and cowardice, you might have amounted to something, Scott? You might not have been left with the crippling memory of a mother who deserted you in the most irretrievable and irreconcilable manner imaginable. She abandoned her son. Her very own son. With her pious sneering from on high and her misguided moral certitude. Let us talk about cowardice shall we?'

Hunter turned. He was desperate to wound Sinclair, burning inside with the hurt and the betrayal. He wanted to kill him. But before he was able to do anything the giant let fly another vicious blow connecting with Hunter's already bruised kidneys, dropping him to the floor. He clutched his sides and curled into a tight ball to stop the searing pain. Sinclair hitched up his light linen trousers and crouched beside him.

'I know all about you and your weak little family, do you see? You're poor mother simply didn't have the stomach for it.'

'Stop it,' David cut in. 'There's no need for this.'

'David, please tell me he knows why his pathetic excuse for a mother took her own life?'

'Stop it now. Scott, don't listen to him.'

'You haven't told him, have you? Oh David, have you been protecting him all these years? With what, with a pack of silly lies? That was always your mother's failing Scott, she was unable to embrace the truth, however awful that might have been. Now, I would like you to tell me all of the names on both lists, please.'

Hunter had started to sit up, still clutching his side. 'I know your father's one of them. Seidel!' He spat out the name, hoping to shock Sinclair.

The professor's laugh was one more of exasperation. 'Yes, I think we're all aware of my father. The other names, Scott. The *other* names. Now please, if you don't mind?'

'No.'

'Very well,' Sinclair looked at the giant. 'You have fifteen minutes to tell me all of the names on the second list.'

'Or what?'

'Or your father bleeds to death in the most unpleasant manner.'

The giant's gun jerked once and David slumped to the floor.

'You will understand, and I am no great authority in such matters,' Sinclair continued calmly, 'but people who know about such things,' he nodded towards the tattooed killer, 'tell me a wound such as that, to the stomach, normally takes about fifteen minutes to finish a man. It's not an exact science of course, so you'll forgive me if he bleeds to death a little sooner. Once I have the lists, you are free to go and take your father with you. Mount Auburn Hospital is not far. I shall not ask you again though. The names, please.'

'You mustn't tell him, Scott,' David groaned.

Hunter knelt by his father. The dark crimson patch of blood on his shirt and cardigan already spreading quickly. David Hunter clutched his stomach against the pain and held his son's eyes, steering his gaze lower. Scott thought he was looking at his wound but quickly realised his father was staring at something else. The dull metal butt of the Super-Star pistol.

'Someone once told me a father should never see his son with a loaded weapon,' Hunter whispered.

'And when was the last time you listened to anything I said?'

Hunter had to smile. He spun in the kneeling position, the safety still on. Seeing the pistol the giant swung the silenced Glock towards him as Hunter struggled with the sixty-year-old catch. If the monster fired first there was every chance he would hit his father again. Hunter rolled to one side trying to draw the fire away from his father and find cover amongst the rowing equipment, scrambling on his knees, pushing past ropes and buckets whilst he grappled with the unfamiliar weapon. The giant shot and a round sparked off the concrete next to him.

'Stop,' Sinclair shouted. 'Do not harm him.'

The killer turned on Sinclair and for a second Hunter thought he might challenge his superior. In that moment he saw his chance. Discarding the useless pistol Hunter seized an oar and charged at the giant. The Glock puffed and another round buried itself in the concrete floor at Hunter's feet. The giant was raising his gun in his broken hand, but now Hunter had the initiative, he kept moving forward, towards the danger, swinging the oar as he went. A round hummed past him and another, but the giant was backing away as he shot, unsteady on his feet. Hunter's father lay huddled on the floor, unable to help his son, but as the killer backed away from the flailing oar, he stumbled over David Hunter's legs and his son pounced. The oar flashed through the air and caught the giant's throat, ripping through the swirling tattoos and crushing his wind pipe. The hulking figure swayed slightly and collapsed. Hunter had never so much as slapped someone before. He looked down at the twitching, grisly corpse before him amazed at just how little remorse he felt. That, in some small way, was pay back for Amy, Alec and Joth. But it wasn't enough. This man dying at his feet, whoever he had been was only working to Sinclair's orders. Hunter threw down the bloodied oar, picked up the Glock and turned it on Professor Frederick Sinclair.

'Who was he?'

'A kindred spirit,' Sinclair replied calmly, 'of yours.'

Hunter stepped closer.

'Explain.'

'When you have relatives like ours, Scott, in certain circles it is possible to garner a degree of celebrity. But what am I saying? You still don't really know who or what your grandfather was, do you?'

'Go on.'

'Has it never struck you as odd how little you knew of him? Do you for instance have fond memories of the man? Actually, do you have any memories of him at all? I'm assuming not? Why would that be, Scott? How old were you when he died, four, five?'

'I was six.'

'I see. I'm guessing your home isn't littered with pictures of smiling little Scott sat on granddad's knee, playing with a ball in the park, flying a kite or going for long walks in the country? And shall I tell you why that is?'

Hunter looked across at his father. He was bleeding badly and slipping in and out of consciousness.

'Tell me,' Hunter flicked the gun at Sinclair, 'Quickly.'

'I'm intrigued. What exactly was it you thought your grandfather did?'

'He was a chemist.'

'Indeed,' Sinclair nodded. 'There is some truth in that.'

'A good one too. He was brought here after the war.'

'Ah, I see.'

'Wiseman helped him disappear, along with your father.'

'Yes. That's right. And why was that do you suppose, Scott? Why not welcome them both with open arms as the Americans had done with von Braun and Reinhard Gehlen? The vanquished forced to work for their victors. Why do you suppose we chose not to celebrate them as the Americans had done?'

'They had to remain hidden. The Cold War. The Russians.'

'To stop the Russians from what, kidnapping them? Oh Scott, is that what you really think or have you inherited your father's charming naivety?'

Hunter wrapped both hands around the semi-automatic. There would be no mistake this time.

'Your grandfather, my father, they were undeniably great men in their fields. But during the war they made certain choices. They joined the Nazi Party. Well, many good people did, but they *embraced* the Nazi Party. They let it into their hearts, their souls, their very beings. All of the people on that list worked in Hitler's Death Camps. They were torturers, sociopaths, murderers, butcherers and the vilest of human beings. They did things which you cannot even imagine. Unspeakable things and they did them willingly, Scott, on a daily basis and with a clear conscience. Had they not been such gifted scientists they would surely have been tried for their crimes or found with piano wire around their necks hanging from the nearest lamppost, like this man's grandfather.'

Hunter considered the corpse at his feet.

'Some, your mother for instance, might have found that preferable. The Jew, Wiseman was responsible for bringing them here and helping them disappear not because they were great men but because they were quite the opposite, do you see?'

'Who was he?'

'He was nobody, but his grandfather was Otto Kästner. He served at Ravensbrück. Himmler awarded him the Totenkopfring for his work. Look the poor fool still wears it.'

Hunter examined the death's head ring, able to make out the mystic runes clearly now, so not a Hell's Angel after all.

'I met his father at Bayreuth. Our type are always welcome there. He had fully embraced Hitler's teachings, do you see? Not a pleasant individual you understand, but, and I think you would have to agree, not lacking in enthusiasm for his work.'

'I still don't understand why your father's reputation is worth killing for?'

'How ironic. Your mother didn't have that problem. She was so consumed with guilt and shame she couldn't live with herself. If it's any consolation, she wasn't alone. Martin Bormann's son became a priest, poor misguided fool. He could have had the world at his feet. I, on the other hand have a distinctly more pragmatic outlook on life. Whilst I find the whole affair deeply distasteful...'

'Distasteful?'

'I am neither proud of my murderous father's work, like this fool,' he said kicking Kästner, 'nor ashamed. He was him and I am me, we were related, nothing more. I've heard people say you can't choose your parents. A little trite I think you'd agree, but perhaps there is some truth in it? I suppose *you* would argue that we'd have been a lot better off if our respective relatives had suffered the consequences, not to say indignities of the War Crimes Investigation Unit? Anyway, when my father's reputation stands between me and something I truly deserve, well that I cannot have.'

'The deanship.'

'Quite. I mean really, how many deans of Trinity College have a Nazi war criminal for a father do you suppose? Thanks to the Wiseman's rather archaic fondness for secrecy, had the existence of the lists not become known, none of this would have been necessary. I have kept a watching brief on all things Enigma for the last fifty years, on the off chance that something unpleasant should surface. My father you see was convinced the Wisemans had kept some record. He hated both of them. Not just because they were Jews but because they held that over him, the lists I mean. I was horrified and deeply sorry the morning you showed up with that code. I knew what it must be and I knew I must prevent it from ever becoming public and at any cost. So you see I'm afraid all of this is very much your doing, Scott?'

'Would you have silenced the others?'

Sinclair thought for a moment, as though he were considering a particularly irksome crossword puzzle or struggling to recall a student's name. 'Yes, if it had become necessary.'

Hunter didn't know what to think. He looked at his father. The colour had drained from his face and he was shaking violently. He had to get him to a hospital and quickly.

'Scott, do one last thing for me. Leave the gun.'

Hunter found a table by the door. He was about to lay the Glock down and present Sinclair with the easy option, the path Wiseman had chosen, unable to confront his past and his part in Amy's death, the path his mother had chosen, unable to confront her father and his past.

No.

He turned and marched straight at Professor Frederick Sinclair firing as he went.

'How's this for sentimental you fucker.'

The first round tore out Sinclair's throat, Hunter following the body as it descended towards the floor, the second cracked his sternum and as Sinclair hit the ground the last bullet struck him precisely between his eyes. One for each of his victims.

As Hunter carried his father from the boat house a blacked out Audi A4 pulled up. Bennett and Healy had received the text Hunter had sent from his father's house. Hunter caught Healy's eye. There it was again, that look of practised indifference, but this time Hunter thought he detected something else. Was that a hint of grudging respect, a glimmer of admiration?

'They're in there,' Hunter said nodding grimly towards the boathouse. Neither Bennett nor Healy replied. Just business.

He placed his father carefully on the back seat of the Volvo, found an old travel blanket to

cover him with and set off into the night.

12

Hunter spent the days before the funeral in Fellows' Gardens. He'd always thought if he were to propose to Amy he'd do it there, beneath the cherry trees, when they were in blossom. Now he went there to drink and contemplate. The rhododendrons had shed their beautiful flowers, they lay in an ugly carpet of faded pinks and browns, slowly decomposing into the borders. The plant would come again. Next year, it would be stronger if it were well cared for, perhaps more beautiful still.

He spent long hours considering Wiseman's parting statement to him, seeking to comprehend what exactly the old man had meant. What had been the nature of his terrible mistake? Had it been a mistake to help and thereby involve Hunter? Was he trying in someway to atone for Amy's death? Then there were the five men and one woman who should have stood trial but had instead been deemed too valuable and so had been spirited away by the Wisemans, perhaps that had been George's greatest offence? And always in the background the sense that the real fallacy hadn't been George's at all, but his father's?

Hunter thought long and often about his own crimes. Had it been wrong to kill Sinclair? Had it brought back Amy or the others? Had it made him feel any different, any better? Fleetingly perhaps, but ultimately there had been no satisfaction in the act. In fact, Hunter had been surprised how little he had felt at the ending of another human being's life and that had troubled him more than anything, the formidable persona of his grandfather now ever present. Could he have inherited some of his distant relative's disregard for humanity, for the sanctity of life?

With Sinclair's murder Hunter knew he would be forever changed. He had taken another's life, that could not be reversed and he had done so in the most personal and intimate of manners. He wasn't certain of the details of his grandfather's time in the concentration camps. It was possible, he supposed, that he had watched the slaughter of innocents from afar, an interested spectator, but that didn't make him any less guilty, any less culpable. Hunter had actually killed, with his own bare hands. He was, and always would be, a murderer.

He met Mr and Mrs Proctor the day before the funeral. They had taken him out for lunch to give them a chance to talk. He'd had to fight his new found instincts to drink before and during the meal. Afterwards, well that had been a different matter, there had been no one to prevent him then. He went back to the house and found a bottle of whisky. Bottles of whisky or at least half or quarter finished bottles were easy to come by since his confrontation with Sinclair.

Her parents had said they understood he had nothing to do with her death, that he shouldn't feel guilty, but he knew they didn't mean it. The instant he'd seen her mother's face he'd known she held him completely responsible for her only daughter's death. It hadn't upset or surprised him, not really. Why would it? He *was* responsible for her death. Her father had seemed a little more understanding, if that was the word, but Hunter expected this was in part due to the shock he was obviously still suffering. Fathers and their daughters.

Hunter opened the front door and entered the empty house on Danforth Road. Sartre had said that hell was other people. Well Sartre had been wrong. Signs of recent events were still very much in evidence. Loops of blue and white police flutter tape hung loosely, furniture and fittings had all been disturbed in the intensive police investigation which had followed Joth's murder. Windows, tables, any surface still bore the remnants of the white powder they had dusted with. Hunter simply hadn't had the energy nor the inclination to tidy up. He pulled down his tie and undid his top button. His suit wasn't quite black, but it was dark and he'd had no money for a new one. He shuffled into the hall, taking off the jacket as he went, in his hand a supermarket bag heavy with cheap scotch and cigarettes. In the kitchen cups and plates piled on the table as they had been the week before. The paper Joth had been flat hunting from had fallen to the floor where it remained.

He put the bag on the kitchen table, next to the Glock. He'd toyed with the idea of ending it all of course, on one occasion going so far as to rack the slide and place the gun's cold barrel in his mouth. But then he would have been no better than Sinclair, worse perhaps. Afterall Sinclair's life had been drawing to an unpleasant close, but Hunter's was just beginning, although a less auspicious start he was struggling to imagine.

He found a teacup in the sink. It was dirty but empty. He rinsed it quickly under the cold tap, before running his index finger around the rim, rubbing away the stain, then he poured himself a healthy slug of whisky. Gone all the mystique and romance of the drink. Hunter hardly even noticed the taste anymore. That was not why he drank. It could have been anything he poured into the cup as long as the numbing sensation was there too. Soda, ice, neat, he'd given it no thought, no consideration whatsoever. It went into the glass and he threw it down his greedy throat as quickly as he could fill the next one. He took the bottle through to the sitting room hesitating at the spot where he had found Joth's body. Another large gulp from the teacup.

On the welcome mat lay a brown manila envelope. Hunter regarded it through tired, bloodshot eyes. He hadn't the strength, the will nor the courage to pick it up. He took another drink. Perhaps if he drank enough it would go away?

In the sitting room he sat and stared at the antique Anniversary clock his father had so lovingly restored. It took pride of place on his mantle piece. An obscure reminder of his parents from a time he didn't recognise and a man he barely knew. The whisky bottle slipped from his grasp and came to rest on the carpet between his feet.

He had not imagined it and it would not go away. He would have to deal with the envelope which threatened to dominate his house and his life. He rummaged in the bag and found some cigarettes. He'd smoke one first before venturing into the hallway. He hadn't smoked since his first year at university, but now he couldn't think of any sensible reason not to.

The envelope lay face down. Hunter picked it up and examined it. With a horror of recognition he realised it was exactly the same as the one which had brought him the code. The same neatly typed white sticker and the same absence of postmark. That meant someone had waited until he was home to deliver it and they could still be outside, but deep down Hunter knew they weren't. That wasn't the way these people, whoever the hell they were, worked. He slipped his finger under the flap and peeled it open. A quick glance was enough to tell him it was not another code. They looked like photographs. Black and white photographs, perhaps thirty in total. He was going to need another drink. He took them back into the sitting room and sat on the floor next to the whisky bottle and makeshift ashtray, his back propped against the sofa. The envelope's contents fell to the floor where they fanned out, the slick surface of the paper sending them skidding chaotically over one another.

Before him lay a pictorial history of the previous seven days. There he was standing on the doorstep of the house, in his hands an identical envelope to the one he currently held. Another of him bounding up the steps to Wiseman's flat in Kensington. Then with the old man in Hyde Park and there, lit only by the porch light, he was waiting to be admitted to his father's house in Sarratt. Then he saw the sequence of Amy. The pair of them arriving in Kensington, the morning she had disappeared and the moment her life had ended. Hunter couldn't take it all in. He hurled the teacup across the room. Who was playing this macabre game with him? Why had they chosen to ruin his life, strip him of everything he held dear? He clutched the photographs close, trying to gain some last contact with Amy.

As he sat, surrounded by the remnants of his life, the house phone rang. He brushed away a tear, wincing as the scar at his eyebrow bit and burnt and grabbed the telephone from the table where it lay. Resuming his position on the floor he lifted the receiver.

'Mr Hunter?'

'Who is this?'

The voice on the other end of the line was cultured and considered. Hunter imagined its owner had probably been to one of London's more exclusive private schools, then, no doubt independently wealthy, had spent his life smoking expensive cigars and drinking expensive brandy. He also had the distinct impression he'd heard the voice before.

'Hello, Mr Hunter. This is Lazarus. Please don't put the phone down. I'm sorry to bother you at such a time. As you can no doubt see I have been following your progress with a considerable degree of interest.'

'Who are you?'

'I am a friend, Mr Hunter, that is all I can tell you. I believe at this time you may be in need of a friend and I'm not talking about the kind you find at the bottom of a cheap bottle of whisky.'

'You followed me?'

'Yes,' Lazarus's voice rumbled.

'Why didn't you help? If you're a friend, why didn't you help us?'

'I'm sorry, I was not in a position to help you. Events, tragic though they undoubtedly were, had to be allowed to unfold. I am offering you my help and friendship now though.'

Hunter took up the bottle by his feet, unscrewed the lid and drank. 'Go to Hell.'

'I do understand.'

He had to struggle not to laugh. Nobody could understand where he found himself now. Nobody.

'Scott, you should know that we are grateful for everything you've done. In fact we are in your debt.'

'We. Who's we? Who are you?'

Appearing not to have heard, Lazarus continued, 'I am going to make you an offer. I shall make it once and if you reject it you will not hear from me again. I would very much like it if you would come and work for me.'

'Doing what?'

'Again, I am sorry Mr Hunter, but that information is strictly need to know.' The phrase the old man had used. 'Let me just say that whilst I have been observing you I have been greatly impressed by some of your talents...'

'Go to Hell.'

'and believe you would be a considerable asset to our organization.'

Silence.

Hunter was about to put the phone down. He looked around him. He was sitting in a crime scene, he was drunk and alone and he knew what Amy would have said.

'I'm sorry you do not feel able to work for me, you shall not hear from me again. Goodbye, Scott.'

'Wait, wait. All right, I'll take your job.'

It was Lazarus's turn to hesitate.

'I am very glad to hear that, Scott,' he said after a long beat, and then the phone went dead.

In his office on the South Bank, Sir John Alperton allowed himself to smile. He tried to remember when he'd been Hunter's age, to recall a time before the strain of ambition, the mendacity of work and the constant dissemination. He tried to remember if he had been quite so strong, quite so courageous. He closed the file marked *Sinclair* and threw it on top of Wiseman's. Bridget would know where to dispose of those. A crisp new folder lay open and waiting. In went copies of the photographs and the code he had sent Scott Hunter. Then there was Wiseman's manuscript, that went in as well. Closing the file he took a key and opened the secure drawer at the bottom of his desk. None of this, he reasoned, need trouble Bridget nor anybody else, not just yet.

I hope you've enjoyed reading

Birth of a Spy

Could I ask you to please leave a review, however short.

Thank you.

Printed in Poland
by Amazon Fulfillment
Poland Sp. z o.o., Wrocław